TALES OF SPACESHIPS AND MAGIC

KATE MACLEOD

CONTENTS

REQUIRED TO ASSIST

Shifting from a lack of awareness of anything to a vague feeling of warmth and comfort is not really waking up. And I guess I was half-sensing someone calling my name, but that warmth was so, well, comforting, I just wanted to sink back down in it.

And then my sinuses filled with the assault of ammonia and I was up, not just awake but sitting up, pushing the offending source away from my face as I struggled to scramble back from it. That was harder to do than it ought to be, my muscles still lax from the long hibernation, my joints not as young as they used to be. So I just flailed.

"Miss Lorna, please be calm."

The voice had an odd tone to it, a deep yet vaguely female voice, but too deliberately soothing. I had opened my eyes when the ammonia fumes had hit me, but it was still too bright to see, and I was blinking madly, trying to decide between the pain of eyes open and the confusing lack of information of eyes closed.

I was still flailing. Someone was near me, someone was assaulting me with horrible smells, and yet I didn't know where they were.

"Please be calm, Miss Lorna," the voice said with more urgency. "I do apologize for startling you. Often if I remain motionless for too long humans forget that I am there. I have startled many people, I am sorry."

"Get rid of the smell!" I all but shrieked.

"It is already gone. Just take a few deep breaths, Miss Lorna."

"Don't call me that," I said, but I stopped flailing. I threw my legs over the side of the metal table I was sitting on – not cold, there must be a heater beneath it keeping it at just the right soothing temperature – and let my head fall forward then slowly opened my eyes. No longer staring straight into the lights, they finally had a chance to adjust. A field of white came into focus, then I saw the speckles of shiny gray embedded in the white and realized I was looking at the usual flooring of a medical bay.

"Would you prefer Miss Wincott?"

"Lorna is fine," I said. "Just Lorna. No miss." I raised my head to see narrow feet in shiny white boots. My gaze traveled up past the knees where the boots didn't end, then past the hips that still seemed to be covered in shiny white pleather. At that point I stopped trying to make sense of it, some androgynous form covered in pleather, but when I reached the shiny, white head, the features merely suggested by indentations in the planes of the face – no mouth or to eyes or ears or nostrils to speak of, just bumps and indentations to suggest where such things might be – my brain finally settled on android.

"How are you feeling, Lorna?" the android asked me, leaving just the slightest gap before my name so I could still feel the "miss" there.

"I'm all right," I said, running my hands over my face then through my inch-long hair. They had cut it short just before they had put me in hibernation. That felt like minutes ago. "Why am I awake?"

"There has been an incident which triggered the protocol to rouse you," the android said.

"Protocol," I repeated. I wish it would find smaller words. I didn't know how many decades I had been asleep, but the brain fog was lingering something fierce.

"Are you having memory difficulties? Do you recall the agreement you signed with Generations Corp?"

"I recall," I said with a sigh. The only way I could afford a ticket on this ride to a new world: I had volunteered to be the emergency responder for the flight. If a problem arose that the ship's computer systems could not resolve, it was programmed to wake a human. In this case: me.

The training had been… interesting. It spanned a week, but somewhere in the second day, my trainer looked up from his materials to say to me, "you realize of course that everything I'm telling you the computer already knows how to resolve? Anything you'd be roused to deal with is frankly beyond our ability to predict."

At the time I had taken that as meaning there was little likelihood I'd be awakened at all, and he had agreed it was a remote possibility.

And yet here I was.

"Would you like to see the data we've collected for you, Lorna?" Again with that little pause. Data. That sounded like a good place to start. I had compiled data to earn my paychecks back on Earth. Not terribly exciting work, but it had paid the bills.

"Yes, the data," I said, but then, "You know what? In a bit. First I need tea. A proper cup of tea."

"I shall fetch one for you," the android said.

"No," I said, finally raising my head to look right at its expressionless face. "No, just point me in the direction. I'll make my own."

"Are you ready to walk?"

I pushed off the table, my stocking feet hitting the floor. I was a bit wobbly at first, but a few steps in I had it.

The android had a smooth, gliding gait like a debutante from another age who had practiced for years walking with a book on her head. It was also fast, slipping past me to take the lead which was just as well since I didn't know where I was going. I kept a few fingertips brushing against the wall in case my balance abandoned me, but I found myself getting stronger the more I moved. The effects of some of the stimulants I had been given during the rousing procedure, I remembered that much from my training.

I had been put under while still on Earth, the sleep coffin with my body in it being launched up into space and slotted into its spot on the generation ship while I was already sleeping the sleep of the next-to-dead. I had seen brochures but hadn't paid much attention to them. I had been the last passenger to sign on, the ship unable to leave for its colonial destination without a person willing to be woken in case of emergency and possibly not put under again. People with families didn't want to reach their new home with Mom or Dad suddenly a century older or even dead.

I didn't have a family. I just wanted to get off the Earth, to leave that whole world behind. The details of the ship, even of the world we were heading to hadn't mattered as much as just leaving.

I found the reality of the ship much larger than I had imagined from the pictures I had glanced at. Everything was shiny and white, not just the android, and would be impossible to keep clean if all the humans in its holds were awake and moving around, touching things with their oily hands and filling the air with their dander. Now that my eyes were adjusting the light felt less harsh, more a soft glow that didn't have to work too hard to fill such gleaming spaces. I heard a whirr behind me and glanced back to see a cleaning robot polishing the floor. The sound its motor made was like it was humming to itself while it worked, never quite finding a tune but merrily in search of one.

"We have a variety of foodstuff available for your use, Lorna," the android said. "Here are the teas."

It opened a pair of doors, and I ignored all of the bright, attractive packaging to lunge at the familiar blue and black logo of my favorite brand of English Breakfast. I put two bags in a mug and filled it from the spigot of boiling water then looked about the kitchen for a refrigerator.

"You require something?"

"Splash of milk?"

"Ah." The android opened what looked like another cupboard, but the interior was cooled. I held out my mug, and it carefully poured just a splash of whole milk into my darkening tea.

"Sugar, Lorna?"

"No, I'm good," I said, looking around and finding a sort of breakfast nook in one corner. I slid into the seat and touched the center of the table, which as I had suspected was a computer display. "OK, data now."

"There has been a death among the hibernating humans," the

android explained as medical charts and video playback feeds frozen on the first frame filled the tabletop. "A young man of 22, sudden heart failure. Rare, but not unheard of. But our statistical analysis indicates the likelihood of natural causes and that of foul play are close enough to equal to trigger a waking protocol."

"Our analysis?" I looked up at the android as I took a first cautious sip of tea.

"The ship's computer and I run different processing systems. This allows us to collaborate without merely duplicating efforts."

"I see," I said, glancing back down at the data. I was no medical doctor, without the red, green and yellow bands I wouldn't know what was abnormal, normal, or borderline, and even with the bands, I didn't know what any of it meant. "Do you think it's likely I'll see something you missed?"

"The situation triggered the protocol," the android said.

"Okay then," I said, taking another sip of tea. "What do you recommend I do first?"

"You can examine the body or the hibernation pod," it suggested.

"Let's look at the body first," I said, shutting down the tabletop display and sliding back out of the booth. I don't know if it was the stims finally kicking in or those first few sips of tea, but I was feeling more like I was refreshed from an afternoon nap rather than groggy from hibernation sleep.

"How long was I under?" I asked as the android led me back down the long hallway that was the spine of the ship.

"84 years, 5 months and 12 days," the android replied.

"That long," I said. I suppose my first thought should have been that everyone I had known back on Earth would be dead now, but I had never known that many people.

The android brought me to another medical bay, a clone to the one I had been revived in. It seemed a strange sort of empathy that the android had roused me in a different room. The idea that I could have woken from hibernation to find myself sharing a room with a corpse made me shiver, and I was glad I had dodged that fate.

I had expected to find the murder victim under a sheet or something, but he was just laying on a table, dressed in the same sweatpants and Generations Corp logo T-shirt and hoodie that I was. He had gone without the optional socks, so my first impression of him was that he was one of those people whose second toe was longer than their big toe, which for a moment struck me as funny because the shape of the android's feet suggested the same dimensions. I had the overwhelming need to crack a joke about it or even just start giggling but swallowed it down and took a drink of tea instead.

No need to let hysteria take over just because this was my first encounter with a dead human body.

The android was at the bedside and waiting for me to draw nearer. It suddenly felt wrong to be casually drinking tea, and I looked around until I found a workstation near the doorway where I could set it down. I ran the palms of my hands over the sides of my sweatpants nervously but made myself step up to the body.

Twenty-two. But he looked like just a kid. And a handsome one at that. There wasn't a mark on him, but then if the cause of death was heart failure, there wouldn't be.

"Are you quite well, Lorna?"

"Yes, just fine." I tried to figure out what I was supposed to be doing, what clues I could possibly be searching for. Neither my previous data compiling job nor my brief Generations Corp training had covered any of the skills of a medical examiner or homicide detective.

"I have grief management programming should you require it."

"No, I'm quite fine."

"Did you know the victim?"

"No," I said and gently put my hands on either side of his head to lift and turn it, looking for anything out of the ordinary. He was still supple. I suppose they had chems for that too. "I didn't know anyone on this ship. That's why I'm the one you woke up. I'm not colonizing as part of a family group, and the only way to fly solo was to volunteer for this extra responsibility."

"I understand," the android said.

I ran my hands over the young man's arms, again lifting and turning, and his legs, and had the android assist me in turning him on his side to look at his back. But I saw nothing.

"Let's check the pod then," I said, retrieving my tea.

"This way," the android said. I took a sip of cool tea, now quite on the strong side with the two tea bags still floating in it. "What will you do with his body?"

"He will be returned to his pod when you have completed your investigation and returned to stasis until the ship reaches the colony world. Then the family shall receive it and decide what should be done based on their own beliefs and traditions."

"I suppose, you already had a space for him, no reason not to let him keep using it," I said. The android gave an exaggerated nod, like that was a gesture it had seen but never attempted before.

The end of the hallway was an elevator built to transfer hibernation pods between levels. There were no doors but when the android touched the panel on the wall the floor before my toes developed a fine line that extended to the walls on either side of the hallway. Then the line became a definite split, and then the floor on our side of the split began to descend. It was a slow, gentle descent, but when we had passed below the floor we had left behind I saw an immense cavern below us, faintly lit by the indicator panels of hibernation pods. Row after row, each row stacked more than a dozen high, and nothing to keep me from falling forward off the elevator platform to the floor lost in the gloomy light below.

As if sensing my sudden vertigo the android caught my arm. Its grip was strong but not machine-like. Its pleather exterior was not just shiny; it had a soft give to it. Not like flesh, more like a piece of furniture, but warm. I opened my mouth to tell it again that I was fine, but in truth, the bit of touch, nonhuman as it was, was still comforting and I closed my mouth without saying a word.

As the elevator descended lights began to swell up from twilight to a glow more like the levels they were at above us. By the time we settled even with the floor I could see clearly, but we were below the tops of the pod stacks, so only the row to either side of us was visible.

The android showed me to the pod the young man had been in, fourth level up and six over from the edge of the embankment it was part of. It felt random. The android summoned over a lifting robot, and I climbed into its little cherry-picker box and buckled into the safety harness. I gave the android the thumbs up, and the robot hoisted me up to a position beside the now-empty pod.

Again there was nothing I could see that looked like a clue, but I was frustratingly aware that I wouldn't know what I clue looked like even if it was right in front of my eyes. The robot adjusted my position at my every request, and I examined every centimeter of the space, every tube in and out of the pod and where they attached to the panel at the head of the unit, even the bottom. Nothing.

At last, I had the robot bring me back down.

"I need another cup of tea."

"Certainly."

The android and I went back to the kitchen, and I made a second cup of double-bagged tea then brought the medical data back up on the table screen.

"Well, if there is something wrong here, I'm not seeing it," I admitted at last when I had tossed back the last of the tea. "It's rare, but it really does just look like his heart failed on him."

"I concur," the android said.

"So, what now?"

"Protocol requires a period of at least 24 hours between waking you from hibernation and returning you to it," it said.

"In case something turns up?" I asked, still scrolling through meaningless data.

"For your safety. The stims should be flushed from your system by then."

"Yes, of course," I said, remembering something like that being said at my training. That whole week had become a blur in my memory, but in my defense apparently, that had been nearly a century ago.

"I can prepare you some food. Unless you prefer to also do that yourself?"

"No, food I trust you with," I said. "I'm not picky."

"I understand humans when they wake often prefer eggs. I shall make you a cheese omelet."

"That sounds divine," I said, although that might have been redundant after the loud growl my stomach had made at the word "cheese."

I made myself another cup of tea while the android fussed with the cooking robots. I glanced over the other tea offerings in the cupboard but stuck with double-bagging the English Breakfast. After 84 years asleep, 24 hours awake was no bad thing.

I sat back down at the table and fiddled with the idea of bringing up newsfeeds from home but decided not to. I would be sleeping again soon for another century, no need to catch up on the fate of Earth now.

The android put a plate in front of me, the steaming omelet neatly folded, cheddar oozing out of the seams, and beside that a selection of red and green grapes, sliced banana, and a few wedges of an orange.

"You have fresh fruit?" I said, surprised both by the food and by the fact that the android was sliding into the seat opposite of me, to sit with me while I ate. That seemed oddly social behavior for an android.

"It was frozen until just a moment ago," the android said. "We have contingencies for up to three humans to be awake throughout the entire voyage. Any leftover food will become part of the colony supply when you make landfall. If there is more you should require, please ask, and I shall provide all I can."

"This is perfect, thanks," I said. It ought to feel weird, thanking an android, but even the lack of face on the android wasn't enough to make it feel remote any longer. Its warm tones and considerate manner felt more and more human the longer we were together.

"May I ask a question?" the android asked.

"Sure," I said, cutting into the omelet with the side of my fork.

"Why did you decide to leave Earth? You are the only one on the ship traveling alone. Won't you be lonely on the new world?"

"I never get lonely," I said, stuffing egg in my mouth before I could succumb to the urge to clarify that remark.

"Your file did specify you requested a private allotment of land."

"With animals," I said, mouth still full.

"Yes, with animals," it agreed. It folded its pleather hands on the tabletop and politely waited for me to go on. I swallowed.

"Back home on Earth, I didn't have much. I had enough, but it wasn't much." I popped a grape in my mouth, enjoyed the burst of sweet juice, the slight iciness that lingered in the flesh as I chewed. "I had a one-room apartment in a super tower. My job wasn't much, very dull bureaucratic work I could do from my workstation in my apartment. Mostly I took in animals. Strays, orphans, animals that got lost or left behind. I preferred dogs, but I took in cats and other creatures as well. Just not fish, I didn't have the equipment for that."

"You like caring for animals." The android's face was as expression-less as ever, but I felt like the end of the sentence was floating between us "more than for people." I ignored it.

"Yes. Some of the animals stayed with me permanently, but most I just helped through a tough time between owners who could no longer keep them and new owners who were eager to take them in. It was sad sometimes, parting ways with animals I had grown to love in such a short time, but mostly I loved it. And, like I said, some of the animals stayed with me forever. Were mine."

"But you're here now," the android pointed out. "I checked our manifests. We have no adult animals on board, just hibernating newborns."

"The ownership of my super tower changed hands. The new land-lord changed the rules. My animals had to go. I couldn't afford to move; there was nowhere to go. Earth, so overcrowded, and I don't make much. I found new homes for most of them…" I stopped, staring down at my plate of half-eaten omelet, bare grape stems, a few remaining banana slices and bits of orange. My vision was getting blurry. I took a long, shaky breath. "I had to… put my best friend down. He was old, going blind and not as housebroken as he once was. I guess it was time."

The android nodded and its hands laced together tightened ever so slightly.

"He was mine, and I let him down. I tried to find a different place to live, tried to find a place for him to go, even for a few weeks so I could keep looking for an apartment for the two of us. People I had done so many favors for before, I guess they didn't feel like they owed me anything…" I stopped, biting down hard on my lip until the tears stopped. "Well, that's why I'm here, heading to the farthest star I could find, and why I'm looking to live alone."

"With all the animals you can collect," the android said, nodding in what I would swear was authentic sympathy.

"All the animals," I agreed. I sat up straighter, about to ask about its programming, so different from the androids I had met before my hibernation, when I gentle chime sounded, like calling the upper classes to dinner on a cruise vessel.

"Oh dear," the android. "There's been another death."

"Death?" I pushed the plate aside, touching the table screen.

"The same as before," the android said, not needing to visually consult what I was looking at. "It looks like natural causes, but it's another young man. Twenty-one this time. Oh dear."

"Is there a problem with one of the chemicals?" I asked, then felt a sudden wave of horror. Were all the hibernating colonists about to die on me one by one?

"No, we ruled that out before," the android said. "I will run the screens again, of course, but we checked."

"I believe you," I said. "Where is the victim now?"

"Still in the pod," the android said. "Come, we can observe the extraction process."

We ran back down the hallway to the elevator and down to the same bay full of hibernation pods.

"How many bays like this are there?" I asked.

"Sixty," the android said. "Both deaths in the same pod."

"Yes, definitely a clue," I agreed. The extraction robots were in the process of removing the body from the pod. The bottom of the pod had handholds molded into it and was rigid; the robots easily lifted it and the body out and set it on a hovering cart waiting on the floor of the bay.

The minute the robot arms were clear I was there running my eyes and hands over the body, but still no signs of foul play. This pod was one level up and rather than wait for the elevating robot I just climbed up with my own hands and feet, examining every bit of the pod, running my hands over the bottom and examining the tubing running into the panel at the head of the pod. Nothing.

I dropped back down to the ground to stand beside the android. It was about half a head taller than me; I had to tip my head back a bit to look up at its face. "I'm not going back to sleep yet."

"No, I didn't think so," it said.

We followed the robots with the body up to the medical bay, and the medical robots performed a perfunctory autopsy, as apparently, they had done before.

"Heart failure," the android confirmed as I marveled how nothing the robots had done had left a mark on the young man's body.

"Within the realm of normal," I said, mostly to myself.

"The odds of it being normal dwindle the more victims we have," the android said.

I blew out a breath. "OK, I need a different tack. Can you send me personal info on both of these two? There must be something that connects them. I'm not going to be any good at finding out how these two died, but I might make some headway into why."

"Certainly. Would you like that here?"

"No, better send it to the table in the kitchen. This is going to require a lot more tea."

"Certainly, Lorna."

The first victim - and now that I was looking at his file I had to admit I had been avoiding learning his name - was Blake Vanson. He had studied agricultural systems at a university in the American Midwest, not unusual in someone his age looking to emigrate with his family. He had three brothers who had done the same and one younger brother who had been in the middle of a mining systems program when the family's name had come up in the lottery, and they had won their slots on the ship.

No criminal record, no history of associations with suspicious people, nothing remarkable about him at all. From what I glanced through of his college years he had been quite popular, well-liked by students and faculty both.

The second victim was named Sean McGuinty. Less remarkable than Vanson only by virtue of being not quite so popular, but he had compensated with slightly higher academic marks.

But the two had attended the same university.

"You have found something," the android said. I started. I had assumed it was analyzing the same information inside of its own head, but apparently, it had been watching my face the entire time.

"Yes, can you bring up everyone with a connection to..." I leaned closer to the text. "Midwestern Agricultural and Mining Polytechnic University?"

The screen filled with new data. There were a lot of names.

"Can you group these by pod?" I asked.

The names color-coded themselves, then flew apart into separate groups on the tabletop.

"Lots of graduates on this ride," I said, leaning back and taking a sip of tea. Yet another cup had gone cold and bitter on me while I was ruminating.

"Perhaps they were exposed to some sort of infectious agent we are not screening for," the android said.

"Perhaps someone at the school had a grudge."

"That is quite impossible."

I bit the end of my tongue. I wasn't going to get into an argument about possibilities with an android; even if I were right, I'd lose the argument of logic. Instead, I asked, "why?"

"Every space inside this ship is constantly monitored. All irregularities are examined by the main computer. If it had seen anything it couldn't account for, it would have flagged it for your review."

I crossed my arms, staring fixedly but without quite seeing at the group of names that shared a university background and a pod with the victims.

"Something could have deliberately been done to them before hibernation, something very slow acting."

"Possibly," the android allowed.

"But anyone back on Earth would be long dead now. So why do this?"

"Everyone not back in Earth would be on this ship and hence would be hibernating. Except for you."

"And I have no connection to the victims." I shot the android a glance, daring it to check my files and verify that claim, but it made no response. "So what now?"

"The purpose of your investigation is not justice," the android said. "The purpose is to stop further harm to the passengers."

"How do I do that if I don't know who's doing this?"

"Why a who and not a what?" the android replied.

"I don't know. Gut feeling, maybe," I said. "It feels like someone with a grievance."

"I will have the medical robots create new screening parameters. We have more information now than we did at launch. We get beams of information from Earth and reprogram ourselves with the latest data, that is what we are designed to do. I shall program the medical robots to search for everything, even things that didn't exist when we launched."

"Good," I said, then a thought struck. "Is that what happened to you?"

"Pardon?" the android asked, pretty much demonstrating what I was asking about.

"I met a few Generations Corps androids during my training. They were barely more than walking, talking computers. You seem more human. You've had updates?"

"Yes, thank you for noticing. I've had several."

"Wow." I just stopped myself from asking if things had gotten better on Earth. The answer wouldn't change anything. I wasn't going back. Still, if people were creating androids with empathy, perhaps they had found more for themselves as well.

Another chime. This time I knew what it meant.

"They're occurring closer together," the android observed even as we started running for the elevator.

"Same pod?"

"Same pod."

A third young man, Steven Fitzhugh. Same school, same program. I let the robots take him up to the medical bay to start the autopsy while I examined the pod. Every inch, top and bottom, even following the tubing to where it ran into the wall.

I stopped with my hand wrapped around the saline tube, pressed flush with the wall. I touched the wall, a thin panel. I found the edges, nearly flush to similar panels all around it, but when I pressed in gently it popped back out against my hands, resting lightly in place until I moved it aside, dropping it inside the pod as I leaned to poke my head past where its tubes joined the largest twists of all the pods to the left of it.

The inside of the paneled wall was a mass of tubes, neatly bundled in ever larger groups, all running to the right and then down to wherever the reservoirs of fluids were stored, reused, recycled.

There was enough room for a person in there. Not much, but someone could crawl around, unseen by ship's eyes, scuttling about making trouble.

"Can we get cameras in here?" I called down to the android.

"I have drones," the android said. "But may I draw your attention to certain logical problems with your theory?"

I hopped down from the pod to stand beside the android. "Such as?"

"A person can access the tubing for any of these pods from within that wall," the android allowed. "But there is no explanation for how a person could have hidden in there since we launched 84 years ago."

"Or why they waited until now to start acting," I agreed. "But it's what we have. Drones?"

"At once, Lorna."

"Have the computer review the video feeds again. Finer search, whatever."

"I understand," the android said. "What will you be doing?"

"I'm going to check these pods," I said. "One by one. Make sure they all contain people. Because I agree no one could have stowed away and hidden for 84 years, and yet someone is running loose on this ship."

"That doesn't seem likely. We have readings on every sleeper in every pod except you and the victims."

"Someone's readings are lying to you," I said, climbing into the elevating robot. "And if they can lie to your medical sensors they can lie to your optical sensors. So I'm going to check."

"As you wish," the android said. Its new more human programming was allowing it to shade that with skepticism. I didn't mind. There was a reason the protocols had triggered waking a human, after all.

Of course, it's one thing to say you're going to check every pod one by one, and quite another to actually do it. Even only searching one of the sixty bays didn't cut the numbers to a manageable number; this bay alone contained 10,000 people.

I could have done the math to figure out how long that would take. I didn't do the math. It took as long as it took.

But I popped open every panel as it passed it, and a few minutes into my search the swarm of drones the android had summoned swooped past me through the open panels into the tube-filled walls. I could hear the soft buzzing of the motors as they swept the interior of the wall, searching every space they could reach. The android offered me a monitor to watch but I left that up to the ship's computer and the android, preferring not to be distracted from my own task of looking sleeper after sleeper in the face, crossing them off the potential killer list, hoping they weren't about to be added to the victim list.

It took more than a day. The android brought me more food, more stims, and more tea. My body could function without rest, but it didn't function normally. My muscles took to twitching and cramping, and bits of my brain kept running faster than other bits could keep up with it and trying to reconcile the two was mentally exhausting.

But the murders had stopped. Whether it was the ever-growing number of open panels or the presence of the drones in the walls, the murderer was lying low. Which suited me just fine.

Then, on the third day, I found the empty pod. I almost thought I was dreaming for a moment, hallucinating from too little sleep and too many stims.

"I think I have it," I called to the android who always waited for me near at hand. The android tipped its head back to direct its blank face at me.

"Pod 14867," it said. "Vital signs normal. Are you sure?"

I almost laughed, the sort of laugh that would start out as a sarcastic bark but end in hysterical giggles. Instead, I just said, "no. I want a second opinion. Can you bring it down?"

"Certainly, Lorna."

The elevating robot brought me down at about the same time, and the android and I stood on either side of the pod, both looking in the plastiglass cover.

"I don't see anything," the android said.

"Good, because I don't either," I said.

"But the health indicators are showing no signs of tampering. There is no sign of a loop in playback, nothing suspicious."

"Tell me who this is, send his files up to the table in the kitchen. If I know who he is, maybe I can figure out how he's doing it. But keep the swarms in the hunting. If we have him cornered somehow, I don't want to lose that advantage."

"Yes, Lorna."

I made yet another cup of tea and took it to the table. Gil Templeton. Another graduate of the same program, but interestingly he had transferred into the program midway through. He had been studying much higher level systems management, like citywide computer network stuff, at a neighboring university but then inexplicably a month into his junior year he had transferred. He had taken more than a full course load to make up the time and had succeeded in graduating the same class as the three victims.

Why?

"Android, can you access the social media accounts of these people back on Earth?"

"No," it said, and I slumped with my chin back on my hands to come up with the next idea before it continued, "but the passengers brought many mirror programs with them. They would continue using versions of the same programs but only amongst themselves."

"Well, since they're all here, that's perfect. Show me anything that connects these three with this guy," I said, touching the file names.

I wasn't entirely surprised when what winked to life before me on the table top was the face of a pretty young woman. Long dark hair, dark brown eyes and a genuinely friendly smile that made the corner of her eyes crinkle and her head tip just a bit to one side. The sort of person even someone like me felt more comfortable within less than a minute after hello.

"What's the connection?" I asked, scrolling through her file. "Monica Silas. Same school, same major..."

"She dated the three victims at one point or another during her time at the school," the android said.

"But not the missing body fellow? Gil?"

"There are indications that she has removed things from her social accounts before migrating them over to the Generations Corp servers. Perhaps he is one of the removed things."

"Or maybe she never knew he existed at all," I said. "What about his accounts?"

"He didn't bring any. No social accounts, no e-mail, nothing."

"Odd."

The android made a sound I would swear was a doubting "meh."

"Not odd?" I asked.

"One of his areas of focus, before he transferred, was security. We have noticed more cautious behavior in passengers who have studied such things."

"Paranoid, maybe?"

The android didn't offer an opinion on that.

I tapped my fingers against the sides of my mug, then tipped my head to the side and asked, "do you think his background gives him the ability to spoof your monitors? He made himself appear like he was there when he was not."

The android interlaced its fingers on the table in front of it. "None of the classes he took would have taught such things, but the remarks his professors included in their evaluations of his work indicate a student who spent extensive time studying things that were not on the curriculum."

"So that's a yes?"

"It's a possibility, yes."

"Now that you know what to look for-"

"The computer is already on it," the android told me. "He did not attempt to spoof our visual systems to make us think we were seeing him still sleeping in his coffin. But he must have hidden himself from view when he climbed out."

"And that must have happened recently."

"Yes, here," the android said, lifting its hands from the table. "The computer has traced the likely point in time when he left his pod. Watch the playback. It's on high speed; if you see something, I don't then stop the playback."

I leaned in to watch. Nothing seemed to be moving even at high speed, but I was watching video from the top of the bay gazing down on the faces of the top row of sleepers, sleepers who had been asleep for decades, sleepers who never moved. Only the indicator lights flashing too quickly to read gave any indication as to the passage of time.

Then I saw myself on the video and knew we had gone too far.

"Rewind it, further. Play it again," I said. "Normal speed."

We played it a third time at a slow speed, but still, I saw nothing. How had he gotten from his pod to the inside of the wall without being seen on camera? And the ship had lots of cameras.

"The computer is researching ways people have done this," the android told me. "It is testing itself for signs of any of those methods of tampering. There are many. It will take time."

"And the drones?" I asked.

The tabletop became an array of tiny displays, all focusing on dark, tube-filled corners. Dust, a tool dropped during the ship's construction, but nothing useful.

"OK, so we wait," I said, getting to my feet to make more tea. "He waited 84 years to wake up. Is that possible?"

"There are drugs that will activate over time and wake you out of hibernation," the android said. "At the time we launched they were very primitive. Not reliable."

"Which would explain the random gap of years. He might have intended to wake right after launch, or right before landing, but the timing was off, and he woke up now."

"That's possible," the android conceded.

I brought my tea back to the table and summoned up his file once more. Gil Templeton. Not a bad-looking kid, but he looked like any conversation with him would get uncomfortably intense, fast. Something about his eyes, so focused, just a shade closer together than normal. Like he was fixed on a goal, not to be deviated.

He must have known the three young men he had killed. Had he known Monica?

I brought up Monica's social interactions and tried searching random keywords: Gil, Gil Templeton, creepy, intense, stalker. But if she had ever mentioned him, it had been in the part of her interactions that she had deleted.

"We found the exploit," the android said suddenly enough to make me jump. I had forgotten I was not alone.

"And fixed it, I hope."

"Yes. He could not make us see him when he was not there; he was trusting that when his readings never deviated from normal, there would be no need for us to make a visual inspection. He only needed to make himself invisible to our eyes."

"Only," I repeated. "But you can see him now."

"We cannot make him appear on the archival footage. The problem is with the data collection, not processing."

"Okay."

"But if he passes in front of a camera now, we'll see him."

"Even the drones?"

"Even the drones."

I was too anxious to sit back down, just watched as the drones intensified their search over areas they had already covered, back when they were unknowingly blind. I thought I saw a flurry of motion but before I could even ask the camera view changed and I was once more looking at the overhead view of the bay.

This time I could see the definite image of a wiry thin man climbing out of one of the open panels. His thick, curly dark hair was cut close now like mine, and everyone else's on the ship, and he was wearing the same pajamas, but there was no mistaking those eyes.

"He might have a weapon," the android said.

"Maybe, but I don't think he's dumb enough to use it. He knows you can see him now. He knows something has changed. He's been very careful to not leave a trail of evidence. He was hoping to get away with this."

"I don't see the relevance to this with regards to your safety."

"Just let me talk to him," I said.

"Why?" the android asked. "If we put him back into hibernation the deaths will stop. The problem you were roused to solve will be dealt with."

"Maybe," I said. "But maybe I'm wrong about the why on this. I want to be sure he's not part of a group acting for entirely different motivations, that someone else might wake up and kill more or might already be awake and we don't know because we stopped searching for empty pods. I want to be sure."

"For the safety of the passengers."

"Yes," I said, heading for the door then changing my mind and going back for the tea mug first. I had been drinking from the same mug since I had woken up days before, rinsing it out from time to time but never properly washing it. The ghosts of drips of tea past had left their trails down the sides, especially around the handle. Gil might know exactly how long I had been up, but he couldn't know if I'd been awake before, maybe several times before.

It couldn't hurt to look like more of a part of the ship, more of an authority figure than I actually was.

I heard the elevator running and leaned in the doorway, blowing on the tea that was already quite cool enough to drink. He came around the corner just as I was taking a sip, saw me standing there, and raised a wrench threateningly high.

So, more than one tool had been dropped behind the walls. Typical.

"You're not going to hit me with that," I said, mouth still close to the rim of my mug. He had been advancing, but my statement seemed to give him pause. "Come on, sit with me for a minute. Keep your wrench if it makes you feel safe, but hold it low, all right? We're just going to talk. Tea?"

"What? No," he said. I shrugged. Then I did the hardest thing I had ever done in my life: I turned my back on him. I knew the ship was watching. If he seemed dangerous, it had defenses, not the least of which would be slamming the hatch to the kitchen shut between us. Still, there was always the possibility he'd get the brilliant idea to throw the wrench at my head. I'm not sure the ship could react in time to save me from that.

But he didn't. I sat at the table and he, after a bit of shuffling about, sat across from me.

I took another sip of tea and set the mug down on the table.

"So. I gather this is about a girl," I said.

"It's about more than a girl," he said. The wrench was still in his hand, his grip white-knuckle tight.

"Did you want to explain it to me, or...?"

He just scowled at me. He had said 'about more than a girl,' not 'this has nothing to do with a girl.' I wasn't good with reading people, but I didn't think I was wrong about his motivation.

"Fine, don't talk," I said. "I already know what you're going to say anyway. 'She broke my heart' blah blah blah. Whatever."

He flushed crimson, gripped the wrench tighter still, but said nothing.

"Yeah, you really don't have to say a word. I know I don't want to hear it. Get back to me in a decade or two when your heart's been broken so many times you just give up trying to connect with people. You give up, and you just settle for what little you can have, a shitty little apartment but room enough for you and your dog and some other furry friends. And you tell yourself, 'this isn't so bad. I'm making life a little better for these things, anyway, and they surely appreciate it.' Right? But of course, you can't keep that."

"I'm not talking," Gil said.

"No, you're not. You're listening."

"I don't have to listen to you. Go ahead and arrest me or whatever, but I don't have to listen to this."

"Arrest you? I'm not an officer of the law. I'm a fellow passenger."

"So I don't even have to sit here," Gil said.

"I guess not, but what else are you going to do? We're a century gone from Earth, a century away from the colony. The ship isn't going to help you get back into hibernation. So what's the plan?"

Gil gripped the wrench tighter, so tight it must have hurt because he finally noticed it there, in his hand. He set it down on the table and placed his hands palms down on the surface to either side of it, fingers spread wide.

He took a deep breath.

"She-"

"Oh stop," I said. "I couldn't be less interested."

"But she-"

"No."

"But you asked!"

"I guess I was feeling polite. The moment passed." I took a sip of tea.

"But don't you need to know? For your report or whatever?"

"Again, not an officer of the law. I just make sure the passengers are safe, and I can go back to sleep. I imagine I can do that just as soon as this tea is done." I took another sip.

"The timing of the drugs was off," he said.

"Yes, I gathered that."

"But it still doesn't matter. We'll wake up together when we reach colonial orbit, and they'll all be gone, and it will be just her and me, and it will be fine."

"Yes, you're very original, and I'm sure your master plan was about to go down exactly like that," I said, ignoring the ever-deeper tones to his crimson cheeks. "And you had a plan to get back into stasis?"

"I'm not telling it to you now," he grumbled.

"Oh, keep your secrets," I said. "The ship can see you now. You're trapped. And I'm already sick of your company."

"Then I have no reason not to kill you," he said.

"No, I sup-" was as far as I got before he was suddenly on his feet, wrench in hand. I peered up past the brim of my mug and saw that long piece of metal, round on one end like a femur bone, come whistling through the air for my head.

I had a momentary thought: how ironic that my inability to talk to people was going to be my undoing.

A briefer thought: this is going to hurt.

And I winced. But the blow never came.

Gil shrieked in frustrated range, and I opened my eyes. The android was standing behind Gil, holding him up in the air by one pleather-fisted grip around his wrist. The wrench fell to the floor with a clang, but the android kept lifting, Gil dangling by one arm, feet nowhere near the ground.

"I do apologize for startling you," the android said. "Often if I remain motionless for too long humans forget that I am there. I have startled many people, I am sorry."

It was hard to tell over Gil's screaming and cursing, but I swear it was being sarcastic.

"You can't do this!" Gil yelled. I trust the look of disgust I threw his way communicated all my feelings well enough. I was done talking to him.

"What shall we do with him?" the android asked.

"We?"

"The decision should be reached jointly between computer and human, so we know it is valid. We can put him out the airlock."

Gil grew suddenly silent. He was a loathsome human being, but at least he didn't start trying to bargain or plead for his life. Or perhaps he sensed I might space him just for being so annoying.

"It's tempting," I said. "If he disappears, we can say the others really were natural causes. The girl, Monica, will be sad, but with this one still alive, she'll know why they died. She might feel misplaced guilt."

"I am not qualified to weigh such matters," the android said. I barked out a laugh.

"That makes two of us. I guess we put him back in stasis, let the colonial council have him as their first order of business on landfall."

The android turned towards the door. Gil renewed his cursing and screaming, but I went back to the boiling water spigot. Maybe one last cup of tea. It's not like the caffeine was going to keep me up.

I watched on the monitors as the android guided the medical robots in the process of sedating and then returning Gil Templeton to hibernation. I double-checked the systems he had spoofed to make sure everything was cleaned up, but the computer had been there before me, just like the robots in the bay had put every open panel back in its place.

I lingered over my tea, enjoying the quiet solitude of the ship. Not that it was completely quiet, but the low hum of activity – the robots cleaning in the hallway, the machines in the kitchen kicking on and off, the faraway rumble of the drives – made a pleasant white noise.

"I rather like it here," I said when the android at least rejoined me.

"It seems very much your sort of space," the android agreed.

"I suppose I can't just stay awake for the rest of my years. Duty calls and all that."

"You could," the android said, to my surprise. "There is an alternate we could rouse if you are gone. But you don't want to."

"I don't?"

"No," the android said. "You want your own plot of land for you and your animals. Space enough for as many as you like."

I didn't answer. It felt very far away.

And the dog, the dog I had had to say goodbye to, felt so close. It had been 84 years. It had been a week.

"I have seen your dog," the android said. "You had pictures in your personal file."

I didn't trust my voice. I just nodded.

"Irish setter. Yes?"

I nodded again.

"I will go with you to the medical bay, and you will go back to sleep, but when you wake I will be there again, and with me will be a litter of Irish setter puppies. I will let you sleep longer, until the council deals with Gil and Monica grieves, and they all build the community on the planet including the place for you. And only then will I wake you." To me, that sounded like perfection.

"And then what?" I asked. "Will you have to return to Earth?"

"Oh no," the android said. "Earth has no place for me. I am quite old-fashioned and clunky by Earth standards. No, I shall be an old and useless thing."

Like a blind dog. It didn't say it, but we were both thinking it.

"I should be honored if you would stay with me," I said. "Me and my dogs."

"I have never met a dog," the android said. "But they seem very noble beasts."

"They are," I said. I laid back on the table but picked my head up again just before the medical robot jabbed me with the fine needle. "If you need me again?"

"I'll wake you. You and not the alternate. We are partners."

"Partners," I agreed.

The needle slipped under my skin and the world began to waver before my eyes, but I felt that hand, that warm pleather softness around mine. It was the very last thing I felt before I felt nothing at all.

SWORD AND TATTOO

Although geographically we are at the center of the known world, our village is quite remote from the rest of civilization. Few traverse the heart of the Sea of Grass, and those that do seldom venture from the main roads. But on occasion a traveler does go astray. Most of those end up as nothing but bones amid the tall grass that dances like waves in the wind, hidden from sight until they are directly underfoot of the next lost wanderer. Our village is much the same; the small river we settled on the banks of is in a narrow chasm so deep the tops of our few trees are quite hidden. We know it wasn't always this way, that long ago the river created the chasm and we sank down with it, safely out of sight. Now we cannot be found among the nodding waves of grass unless we too are directly underfoot.

So the man who appeared one morning curled up outside the public house's door, half-dead and clutching a broken sword, he was out of the ordinary. He had a wild look to him: long ginger hair in tangled mats, clothes a mismatch of styles and origins from all over the edges of the Sea, face darkened with charcoal to be invisible in the night, the tattoo that dominated his right shoulder blade of two snakes knotted around each other, each biting the others throat with bright red spots of blood like welts on his skin. He could only be a bandit, although one who had strayed far from the usual bandit haunts.

We brought him inside the public house to one of the rooms we had in the back behind the kitchen, places for travelers to stay the night. The public house was older than the oldest of us and our ancestors had made rooms for the comfort of travelers. We never asked ourselves why we still maintained those rooms, even though travelers were so rare, but at least we had a bed to put the delirious, raving man in.

In truth he wasn't the first in our memory to show up in the night for us to find in the morning huddled in the public house doorway, and now we fetched the other foreigner to watch over this one. We called her Nell and she never objected, although she had been old enough when she arrived to tell us her real name if she had chosen. She had not chosen to tell us anything. She had spent twice as many years with us as she had been when she had shown up half-starved and willfully silent. We had fed her but never persuaded her to speak, and she had made herself the one who tended to the public house, keeping it clean and in good repair between our infrequent gatherings.

Now she took to the job of nurse with the same quiet diligence. She washed and bandaged all the man's wounds and trickled honey-water into his mouth whenever his thrashing nightmares desisted long enough to allow it. When he at last woke, she continued to feed him. She of course never spoke, and if he tried to speak to her none of us knew of it.

Then the day came when the man was well enough to walk about. We watched from windows as we spun and wove and across vegetable patches where we crouched weeding as he limped to the edge of the river, two pieces of his broken sword in his hands. He drew his arm back, preparing to hurl the weapon into what depths the river offered. Deep enough to hide the shattered remains of the bridge that had once stood for generations, older even than the public house. They waited, under the dancing current. We felt them there, and anticipated feeling that blade, nestling among the stones, perhaps also waiting.

But then he lowered his hand again, clutching the broken blade so tightly it bit into his palm, his own blood not quite so impressive as that on his tattoo.

The man turned and limped back into the village and found our forge. The blacksmith took the two halves of the sword the man handed him mutely and examined the break. It would take some days to repair. The man nodded and went back to the public house where Nell was waiting. They both disappeared through the doorway and what happened inside those walls the rest of us never knew, but when the sword was repaired the man paid with a gold ring from his own ear. He carried the sword back to the public house and thrust it deep within the thatch of the roof and it was never spoken of again.

The man remained among us, living in the public house with Nell. He seldom spoke, but he said enough to tell us his name was Tore, which was all we needed to know. We showed him a patch of land further downstream where he could grow his own food, and when work that required many backs arose, Tore was always there to do his share.

In the spring Nell emerged from the public house with a girl-child in her arms, a girl born in our own hollow. She was almost one of us. Very nearly, we could tell. The girl had her father's ginger hair but her mother's dark eyes, a startling combination. We stopped by to see her, separately to not startle her parents, and each of us agreed that as well as the hair and the eyes she had something of us, something invisible to her parents but apparent to us. It was something like a smell, something like a feeling as if she were just a bit warmer than another baby might be. We said nothing to Tore and Nell but we were all agreed, she was nearly one of us. And she was a good baby, content to sit on a blanket and play with her own feet while her mother was off fetching water and her father was plucking the feathers from a chicken.

What led the other bandits to our hollow? We will likely never know, but find us they did and before we quite knew what was happening they had found Tore. Tore rushed to scoop his daughter up into his arms and then started for the public house, but one of the bandits cut him off, a shirtless ruffian whose scars were even more extensive than his tattoo. He stood between Tore and the safety of the sturdy door, between Tore and his sword hidden in the thatch. We fancied we could see the hilt just peeping out of the straw, winking in the sunlight. We imagined it glowed like a torch in Tore's mind, like the stones of the bridge never left our awareness.

Another of the bandits, a short wiry lad with a nervous twitch, found the forge and shoved the blacksmith aside, seizing a poker from the fire and striding across the commons to where Tore was holding the others at bay with one outstretched hand, his daughter clinging tightly to the twisted locks of his hair as she looked all around with her great, dark eyes. He didn't see the danger approaching until it was too late. The bandit pressed the hot iron to Tore's shoulder, sizzling through his jerkin to the tattooed skin beneath. Tore cried out, falling to his knees but not letting go of his daughter.

There was nothing we could think to do to help. We could see his sword but could not get it to him, and the other bandits were closing in, blades raised high.

Suddenly a voice filled the commons, a voice making three sounds at once: a high whistle that made our bones shiver, a low but still feminine voice commanding something in a language none of us knew, and between and through the two a scream of pure rage. Air crushed down on us, popping our ears then driving breath from our lungs. Most of us staggered to our knees, a few passed out entirely, but one of us saw Nell enter the commons, moving her hands to compel the air to rush past her, knocking the bandits off their feet. Two little streams of water flowed past her, perhaps from her fallen buckets only the water was flowing uphill. The two streams divided into four, each trickling up to a fallen bandit then becoming a rope of water tying itself around each man's ankles.

Their screams filled our hollow as they were dragged through our little woods, but the river accepted them with a splash and then our normal quiet was once more restored.

Clever woman, did she know? The stones rejoiced, we all felt it; they feasted. Soon even the bones of those bandits would be gone, not a morsel for the fish who avoided the places were the stones of the bridge lay too close together, rolled by time and the current of the river.

Then they would sleep again, they would settle back into waiting. We hoped.

We helped our fallen get back to their feet, but Nell moved not at all, just seethed, her hands in fists, although she had no foes left to fight.

"Nell," Tore said, struggling to his feet with the babe in his arms.

"You told me," Nell said, her voice smooth and melodious, showing no signs of long disuse or even the just-occurred overuse. "You told me one day they would come for you, and I swore to stand by you."

"You did," Tore said, hugging their daughter tight.

"Now I tell you the same," Nell said, finally walking up to him then pulling her hair back, tipping her head so that he, so that we all, could see the little tattoo behind her ear, a circle within a triangle within a circle. "My voice will carry outside of these chasm walls. It will be heard, beyond the shores of the Sea of Grass to the far corners of this world, by all those with ears to hear. My people will come for me."

"And I will stand by you," Tore swore.

We went back to our own business, weaving and weeding, smithing and spinning, but we were in unspoken agreement. When Nell's people came, the child would be in danger, and when the child was in danger not just Tore would rise up. We would stand with him, and so would the stones our ancestors had left to protect us. We feared her people would be many and the stones might not slip back into slumber after that fight. Their hunger would draw them out from under the eddies, up into the air where all with the senses to perceive would feel their presence.

We didn't exactly fear the stones, but we did fear the things so terrible our ancestors had left us hidden behind such fearsome protections, beings so terrible our parents and grandparents had whispered not a single hint of them to us, not even disguised in a fairy tale or parable, and yet we all had been born knowing that fear.

But perhaps it was finally time. Yes, we agreed in silent glances one to the other all around the village. Soon it would be time to come out of hiding, to raise our voices as Nell had risen hers, and face the unnamed thing our ancestors had so carefully hidden us from.

BEING NEIGHBORLY

I guess Sitara IV is a good planet as far as the colonial worlds go. It tends to be hot and humid which Ma in particular hates but I guess that's a good thing for growing crops. The air is breathable, unlike Sitara III where the farmers wear air masks while they work. I'm pretty sure I'd hate that. No, everything around our farm is green, rolling hills covered in row after row of corn, the stalks dancing in whatever breeze they can find. Pa says the green doesn't look right because the constant yellow-gray cloud cover distorts the light. I don't know. I've never been off Sitara IV so I guess I just don't know what green looks like.

Heck, I've only once been off our little farm: the prefabricated house, barn and storage shed that my parents assembled when they first came here. We've added on some expansion packs since then when my sisters wanted their own rooms, snapped together the walls and popped out the doorways. It's not like we're indoors much, my sisters and I. Too many chores on a farm and not enough daylight on Sitara IV.

The short days are a downside of Sitara IV, but all in all it's a good planet for growing things. Which is probably how we came to share it with another colonizing species. We don't even know what they call themselves, but their skin is a sort of olive-green my Pa said looked like jade but Ma says is closer to peridot. I've never seen either of those things except on a computer screen. And anyway most of the colonists just call them the Greens.

We weren't supposed to talk to the Greens.

Pa didn't have to tell me that before he and Ma went into town to sell the harvest and come back with supplies. No need to say, "Pete, look after your sisters. And don't talk to the Greens." I've known since birth we don't talk to the Greens.

It's not like it comes up much anyway. The Greens keep to themselves. We stay on our side of the white markers and they stay on theirs. Sometimes you might see one working their fields, their stooped forms and kind of pointed heads silhouetted against the gray skies, but mostly you don't.

The closest I ever came to one wasn't all that close. I was weeding between the rows of corn on the crest of a hill, the kernels already getting that yellowy smell of ripeness that made my stomach pang despite the fact that I knew it was only good for biofuel. He was kind of mirroring me on the other side, the row of markers smackdab between us in the cleft between the hills.

It was the middle of the growing season, the sun covered by a haze of gray clouds that just seemed to make everything hotter, as if the clouds were pressing down on us. Increasing the heat by increasing the pressure like we learned in school. The air was so full of moisture already it was useless to sweat, it didn't cool you off. Not that you could stop sweating. And the soil I turned up with my hoe wasn't so dry that it couldn't find its way into every gap in my clothing to stick to my everywhere. I remembering wondering how that Green was dealing with it. Had they evolved to better handle the climate on this world we were jointly colonizing?

I paused to stretch my back and, still wondering if he sweated as uselessly as I, I looked his way. He must've noticed me eyeballing him because he stopped too. His stoop was permanent, no way he could stretch that out, but he raised a hand in what I thought was a greeting, although when I raised my own he never put his down. I ended up putting mine back down first so I could get back to work, but I felt awkward as heck.

It takes a day to get to town, a day or two to trade, and another day to get back, and while our parents were away I was in charge. This had been easier when we were all younger. I had had fewer chores and my sisters had been more easily swayed by my authority. But somehow since the last harvest my sister Kenna had sprung up like a weed and seemed to think that since she was taller than me she should be co-boss. After a few loud spats this settled down to her just ignoring me but bossing our little sister Josie around. And Josie, being just five and not knowing any better, Josie loved being bossed around.

So anyways Kenna was out in the yard instructing Josie on the proper use of our laundry machine that sat under the awning outside the kitchen, which she was too little to use on her own anyway. It was an unseasonably hot day, thankfully less humid than before the harvest, and I had left the front and back doors open to let a breeze blow through as I disassembled some machinery and scrubbed the parts clean. The dust of our colony planet was sticky, my Ma once said it was not much like Earth dust at all but more like skin cells and whatnot that used to cling to the vents in the ship she and Pa took here before I was born. I don't know about that, I just know that it's gross and it's bad for engines. This was the first end of harvest where cleaning all the parts was my job. I was being just as meticulous as I knew how. Pa would for sure be checking my work as soon as they got home in another day or two and I wanted it all to be perfect.

The conversation outside about the finickiness of laundry machines cut off with a suddenness that was right unnatural if you know my sisters. For a long moment as I paused, machine part in one hand and tiny scrub brush in the other, straining to listen, the only sound was the soft hiss of loose dirt blowing in one door and out the other. Then there was another sound like nothing I had ever heard before. Kind of like a beep or squeak or something. My parents had shown us lots of videos of home and if this was a sound an Earthly creature made, it wasn't one on any of those videos.

Then Kenna called out, "Pete?"

I set my brush carefully on the lid of the open can of machine cleanser, left the part still dripping with grimy foam on the canvas I had stretched across our kitchen table, and came to stand in the doorway.

My sisters were off to my left, Kenna with a wadded sheet in her hands, one wet end still trailing out from the machine beside her. Josie was standing behind Kenna, faced pressed close to Kenna's hip.

To my right was a Green. I had never seen a Green up close before and had no way of knowing if it was true when folks said all Greens look alike, but I had the eerie feeling that this was the same fellow I had had that encounter with up on our respective hills. I raised a hand in greeting. He fumbled to echo my gesture and that was when I noticed what he was holding in his hands.

I caught it at a funny angle at first, on account of his changing his grip to answer my hello. It looked like some kind of surface elevation diagram, two circles with their outer curves lunging out at me at an angle, each just touching a smaller central circle with four little brown dots in the corners. Four more circles radiated out from the little one, each larger than the last, all overlapping the circles on the sides. Like I said, kind of like a topographical map.

Then he put his hand down, and with both hands - if you want to call them hands; when it's just a thumb and an opposite wider thing I'd call it a flipper - on the object it rotated little-circle-downward and became some kind of basket.

He just stood there staring at us and holding out this basket thing. He didn't even make that meeping sound again.

"Does he want to borrow something?" Kenna whispered to me. It certainly looked like what he was doing. This time of year when none of us had much left it wasn't unusual for neighbors to pop over and ask for some flour or an egg or two. Kenna herself had borrowed corn-meal from the Johnsons to make dinner the night before.

But what on Earth would a Green cross the white line for? And what could he want to borrow in a basket that was more hole than container?

Him staring at us without moving, holding the basket out at arms' length for so long the muscles in his arms must be starting to burn, it began to get awkward. Like that first time we had sort of met.

I was going to have to bend the rule. I was going to have to do something with the Green. It might not be "talk" exactly but I was old enough to know the difference between the letter of the rule and the spirit of it. Any kind of interaction with a Green was the spirit of that rule, I knew that.

But in all fairness he had broken the rules first by crossing the line of markers.

"Kenna, you still have half the cornbread from last night, right?" I said.

"That's for dinner tonight," she said.

"It's neighborly to share," I said pointedly.

She had to think it over, and I knew she was trying to find a point to argue over, but in the end she stuffed the wet sheet back into the machine and tromped into the house. Josie found herself out in the open without cover but seemed to be growing braver. She stepped up to the more meager cover of the beam that held the shading tarp aloft, which also brought her that much closer to the waiting Green. The way she put a fingertip in her mouth to bite at had a nervous, quizzical feel to it, but her blue eyes were wide and curious.

Kenna emerged from the house with the rest of the cornbread carefully wrapped in a tea towel and held it out for me to take.

Fair enough.

I gulped dryly and stepped out of the shade of the house into the hot sun. I immediately broke out into a sweat that wasn't all nerves.

The Green was slick with sweat too. Assuming they didn't always look that way, I found that comforting. For a moment, anyway. As I drew closer I realized that sweating profusely was making me smell rank indeed but the Green, who had been out in the sun much longer, had almost a floral odor, like my Ma's only-on-special-days jasmine perfume but without the spicy undertone. He smelled like a fresh breeze, really. I tried to keep my arms down close to my sides.

His eyes fixed on a point beyond me weren't giving me any hints if I was doing the right thing. I managed something like a smile as I gently laid the cornbread into the basket.

He tutted. That was the actual sound he made. Just like my teacher does at virtual school when I say something stupid. Then he took the cornbread out of the basket, set it back in my hands, and resumed his prior posture.

"Well what on Earth?" Kenna said.

I looked down at the cornbread in my hands then at the Green, who was staring off at something beyond the horizon. It seemed very formal, like he was performing some ritual that involved not looking directly at me. I kept staring and the corners of the Green's eyes twitched like it was fighting the urge to glance my way, but it never gave in.

I sighed. The time had come to break both the spirit and the letter of the law.

"Something I can help you with, neighbor?" I asked. "Can you give us a hint? We're happy to give anything we can spare."

The Green remained as he was.

"They farm like we farm. Do they need some kind of farm thing?" Kenna asked. I wracked my brain. What could fit inside that basket?

I didn't even realize Josie had moved until she was brushing past me to get up on tiptoes and put several of the detergent pods from our washing machine into the outheld basket. They were small and slipped out one by one to fall to the ground.

But I scarcely noticed that, being suddenly keenly aware that the Green likely didn't need detergent, naked as he was.

Or she. I had no way of telling. My cheeks flushed. Whose wouldn't?

The Green bent to pick up the pods one by one and put them back into Josie's hands.

"Pete?" Kenna said again. She was holding out the canister of machine part cleaner. I took it from her and tried putting it in the basket but the Green pulled the basket out of the way, tutting again. Clearly we were trying his patience.

"What else do we have?" I asked. We all went back into the house and looked around. Josie went back out with the neatly folded stack of towels. Kenna, too caught up in the problem-solving to remember to be nervous, went out with a vase of flowers. I rolled up my toolkit in its leather case and brought that out.

One by one the Green rejected our offerings.

We retreated back to the shade under the awning.

"Maybe you should run to the Johnsons," Kenna said. "They haven't gone into town yet. They might know what to do."

"That would take hours," I said. "What could he want?"

The poor Green was getting sweatier, his arms starting to shake from holding the basket up at that height.

"We should invite him inside while we figure this out," Kenna said, reading my mind. "Maybe offer him some sweet tea. Get him to set that down while we think, anyways."

"How?" I asked.

Maybe Kenna and I would have figured out something eventually but once Josie went back out into the yard it was out of our hands. She walked right up to the Green. She stopped to look up at him, hands on hips, head tipped to one side as she squinted against the sunlight. Then she reached out to touch one of his hands. Flippers. Whatever.

And the Green gave her the basket.

None of us knew what to do. Josie turned to look back at us, basket in her hands, but Kenna and I just shrugged. Apparently the Green had come to loan something, not borrow something. But what were we going to do with a basket that wouldn't hold anything useful?

Josie looked up at the Green that was still watching her. She tried to give the basket back but the Green refused to take it. And yet neither did it leave. There was still something it was waiting for us to do.

It was maddening.

Then Josie did what frankly was a very Josie thing to do. She turned the basket over in her hands so that the little brown pegs that would keep the rounded bottom standing up on a flat surface were pointed up into the air like little radio antennae and she put it on her head.

Then she grinned that big Josie grin, turning to face us and point with both hands at the basket on her head.

It's hard to tell with a Green, their lack of noses makes their facial expressions hard to read, but I thought that just for a moment a wave of sadness washed over the Green. But then it seemed to pass and the Green raised its hand/flipper again, facing first Josie, then me, then Kenna, then Josie again. Then it made a little bow and retreated.

I walked to the edge of the yard to watch as it made its way down the hill and between two of the white markers back to its own land.

Josie danced in her new hat. Kenna and I just exchanged a shrug. The situation had concluded itself and there didn't seem to be any reason to worry about it further.

Two days later when our parents came back at midafternoon with a rover full supplies enough to see us through the next season Josie was still wearing the basket as a hat. Ma came around the corner of the house first, arms full of gifts for the three of us carefully wrapped in squares of shiny BoPET foil we'd quickly put to other uses. Josie ran to hug her but Ma fell back a step, all of the gifts tumbling down to the dust as her hands went up to cover her shocked mouth. Josie looked puzzled.

"I have a hat," she said simply.

Then Pa came into the yard, a massive roll of chicken wire balanced on one shoulder. He too pulled up short when he saw Josie in her hat but despite the persistent expression of horror on Ma's face he just burst into great gales of laughter.

"What is it?" Kenna demanded. "What?"

It took Pa a few minutes to get ahold of himself. He stumbled up to hand the chicken wire over to me then went back to fold Ma up into his arms and give her a tight hug.

"No worries, dear," he said as he patted her back. "She's nowhere near the age of consent. This isn't going to come to anything."

"Age of consent?" I asked, eyes moving from Pa's face to Ma's and back again. Neither his mirth nor her shock were abating much.

"Consent for marriage," Pa said. "It's a Green custom. They can be quite insistent about it. A few of the first settlers had to go through a sort of mock marriage with the Greens after quite innocently accepting baskets. Our species aren't genetically compatible but they keep making proposals. It's part of why we put the line up. To prevent those sorts of misunderstandings."

"Marriage?" I repeated, like I couldn't figure out how those syllables made that word, let alone that meaning of the word.

"Don't worry about it," Pa said again. "Now show me my engines."

"Yes, sir," I said.

Ma came out of her stupor and bent to retrieve our gifts, pulling the wrappings tight again. We wouldn't open them until after dinner.

Pa had another fit of chuckles and I gave him a puzzled glance. He waved my look away but then seemed to change his mind and tell me what was funny.

"This Green custom, it's the female Greens that present their tribute to their males," he said. "This one must have gotten confused. Our Josie doesn't look remotely like a male, let alone a full-grown one." He shook his head with another little laugh that I tried to join in but couldn't quite muster more than a soft coughing sound.

I remembered the look of sadness I still wasn't sure was real or my imagination that had washed over the Green's face. Or the more stooped than usual gait he – or I guess she – had had when she had trudged back home. That cloud of despondency that had hovered over her. I was more sure than ever she had been the one who had answered my wave that day on the hill.

I remembered the way she had rested her flipper on the white painted concrete marker as she stepped from our land to hers, the way her flipper had lingered there just a shade too long. I didn't think she was confused. She wasn't going to be coming back, not for Josie.

As we ate roasted chicken and new potatoes and smelled the tart apple pie still cooling in the kitchen, our little harvest celebration feast, I kept glancing over at the modest stack of presents on the sideboard behind Ma.

I hoped when Josie opened her gift after dinner that it was something she absolutely loved. It wouldn't be hard to do; Josie absolutely loved all sorts of things at first sight. But if she did love it, it might be distracting enough for her to set her basket hat aside, to forget about it.

To not miss it when I found it early in the morning and carried it back between the white markers to present it back to its owner. Maybe with a bit of our leftover roasted chicken and a I wanted to show the Greens a human custom or two. Our colonies were young and we were bound to be neighbors for a long time.

TUMBLING UP

he Hydridae on the other side of the glass danced, their willowy appendages tracing arcs through the murky water. Fumahadi nodded and my mother smiled and I realized I was the only one not understanding what was being said.

My heart pounded, certain at any moment I would be addressed, although as an apprentice that was unlikely. Keeping my face blandly polite, I reached up and plucked off the little bindi between my eyes, rubbed the lens carefully on the sleeve of my white silk robe and pushed it gently back into place, also tweaking the translator in my ear for good measure.

"...but where is the other diplomat?" the translator said in its inflectionless voice.

"Other diplomat?" Fumahadi repeated, glancing at my mother, who shrugged. "The League of Worlds only sent us two, plus Nontshaba's apprentice."

"We see a resemblance," the translator said as the Hydridae danced.

"Yes, Nomakhepu is my daughter as well as my apprentice. She is the youngest to pass the entrance exams in a generation and I wasn't ready to part from her," she said with a proud smile. I managed a weak one of my own. The fact that what I had hoped would be my big leap into independence had turned out to be the same life as before with extra chores was not something to even be hinted at in the negotiation room.

"We approve," the Hydridae said. "We also keep our own children close with us. We have met other species who are less concerned with their children. We did not get on well with them."

If the Hydridae had lips, I could imagine them tightly pursed as they made that strange remark.

"If we can return to what you just said about the other diplomat," Fumahadi said. "I am the leader of this diplomatic team, so appointed by the League. I choose who I work with, and they are all in attendance here."

I knew what was making Fumahadi nervous. We represented the evacuated colonists of this water world currently waiting in orbit for us to negotiate for them to stay. But when the Hydridae had come out of the deep to make themselves known there had also been a corporation in the early stages of building a mining station on the ocean floor. Corporations always turned down the League's offer of diplomatic representation, preferring to use their own in-house diplomats. Those were usually disgraced League ambassadors or apprentices who had washed out. As someone with a long history of excellence at the highest levels of the diplomatic corps, Fumahadi did not appreciate being asked to treat such people as her equals.

"Her presence was requested by someone on your side of the table. Surely you were informed?"

Fumahadi's cheeks reddened ever so slightly. The translator was no help in judging tone, and while creatures in constant, supple movement as the Hydridae were doubtless had very intricate and telling body language, we had no way of interpreting it. It could be a simple statement, a reproof, a dig, anything really.

"My apologies, I was not," Fumahadi said.

The Hydridae had built this meeting space in a deep cave under the former colony using the prefabricated building materials the colonists had left behind, so while we sat at a table against the pressure glass that divided our dry side of the room from their wet one, and there was a wall with a door behind us, the floor was a thin sandy layer over cold rock. When the door behind us opened it made a soft hiss over the sand which immediately caught our attention: our third diplomat had arrived.

This new woman wore a white jumpsuit whose austerity echoed the simplicity of our white diplomatic robes, but the deep red shawl thrown haphazardly over her shoulders was deliberately eye-catching. I had a nagging sense of familiarity I couldn't quite place. The little braids dotted all over her head felt wrong to the image my brain was trying to recollect. They were so short they had to be new, as if she were indeed a failed apprentice now free to grow out her regulation haircut.

"Greetings, mistress," she said with a bow to Fumahadi and then I knew her. That deep, mellow voice was unforgettable: Naledi, Fumahadi's former apprentice. Fumahadi had taken her abrupt departure as a cruel betrayal, venting her rage and grief to my mother, her lifelong friend. I could only imagine what it took for Fumahadi to keep all that deep inside, always aware of the watching and doubtless quietly judging Hydridae.

"I was not informed we would have a third ambassador."

"I'm not a third ambassador," Naledi said, crossing the sandy floor to take a chair at the table to Fumahadi's left as I was to my mother's right. "My anonymous employer merely wishes me to observe and advise. Such advice being rendered in private chambers and which you are completely free to disregard."

That sounded like a too-good-to-be-true situation, especially in light of not knowing who she was working for, but in front of the Hydridae Fumahadi merely nodded.

Fumahadi turned her attention back to our hostesses, making formal introductions of each of us in turn. I reached under the table, found my bag and retrieved one of the spare translator units then moved as discreetly as I could down the table to Naledi's side, touching her shoulder. She turned, saw what I had in my hand, and slipped on the earpiece as I touched the bindi between her eyebrows.

"Thanks, Nomakhepu," she whispered then turned back to the Hydridae, who were now making their own elaborate introductions. She nodded to herself then gave me a thumbs up over her shoulder. I went back to my seat, baffled and surprised that she knew my name. As Fumahadi's apprentice she had been on many of the same missions as my mother, but I had been lost in my studies at the time, forgoing most of the outings and recreational events in favor of reading endless texts, only observing the actual negotiations from some far corner. And yet she remembered me.

"May I ask which of you is Kala?" Fumahadi said, our translator having made a complete botch of the Hydridae's complex names.

"The one you call Kala regrets she could not attend. She had very much wished to do so, but is..." the translator hesitated although the dancing of the Hydridae's limbs did not. "...in bud. It is an awkward time for us and would likely be very confusing to you. But Kala has informed us of your ongoing conversation. You may speak with us as freely as you've spoken with her."

The next hour was given over to what was on the surface idle chit-chat. Business is never discussed at the first meeting. Both sides only mouth polite nothings while trying to figure out the tells, how to read the other side before the real work begins. I observed the Hydridae, looking for differences in their dances, trying to discern hints of individuality. I made some tentative notes but doubted I was gleaning much. Hopefully my mother and Fumahadi saw more than I.

Naledi seemed half-asleep.

At last the banquet began. A light beside the small hatch at the end of our table lit up and I got up to fetch the covered trays for each of us.

"The colonists showed us how you prepared your food," the Hydridae said. "It is tricky for us but we built a sealed version of one of your kitchens we can control remotely."

I tried to picture this like hands reaching through the gloves built into a wall like in a lab dealing with toxins or radioactive materials, but dismissed that: not with their noodly appendages. Something more like programmable waldos; I longed to see it. Perhaps later we would be permitted to put on pressure suits and explore their world.

In the meantime there was alien cuisine to try, one of my favorite parts of the job. I lifted the lid and inhaled deeply the aroma of roasted meat. Or was it fish? It appeared to be some round thing about the size of a child's ball. The outside had been glazed with something sweet and brown before cooking; the inside was pink and tasted like shrimp although the consistency was more meaty with a grain to it. The salad appeared to be crisply fried seaweed of some sort, a bit salty for my taste but I liked the bitter tang of the dark greens.

Fumhadi and my mother enthused over the food to the Hydridae but Naledi sat silently, only eating the greens.

"May we eat with you?" the Hydridae asked. "We eat our food fresh and will understand if that is not appetizing to you."

"Please, feel free," Fumahadi said. There was a pause and then a panel opened in the Hydridae's side of the room, filling it with a bouncing school of zooming pink balls. The Hydridae caught them in their willowy arms and brought them to the juncture of their limbs, on top of their tall stalk-like bodies. The balls deflated as they sucked them dry, leaving grayish husks to flutter down to the sandy bottom of the room.

Some of the balls tried to escape or hide in the corners but the Hydridae snagged them all. It was vaguely horrifying watching the pink life get sucked out of them, but I was certain what I was eating was the same creature only killed and cooked first. I glanced at Naledi who hadn't touched hers, but if she felt the same horror at the Hydridae's feasting she didn't show it.

After the meal and more formal shows of politeness we retired to the room prepared for us, really one of the colonists' prefab houses assembled inside the cave. My mother opened and shut cupboards until she found the makings of tea.

"Observations?" Fumahadi asked as she took one of the chairs at the little table. Naledi went to the bunk over mine, dropped her bag on the floor and sprawled out on top of the covers. The house had no roof but the darkness of the cave above.

I glanced at my inadequate notes then set them aside. "I felt like they were observing me more than the rest of you." I used all of my diplomatic training to not let my paranoia show in voice, face or body language but I felt it very deeply.

"You're not wrong," Fumahadi said.

"They were comparing you to your mother," Naledi said, still regarding the ceiling. "Luckily you follow League behavior guidelines as rigidly as Nontshaba does."

"What do you mean?" I asked.

"They do seem a bit fixated in mother-daughter relationships," my mother said.

"They were looking for homogeneity and they found it. They find that reassuring," Naledi said.

"You're guessing," Fumahadi said. "We only just met this species, no one knows anything for sure."

"I'm theorizing," Naledi allowed. "I've been studying these creatures since they made themselves known. Children being very like their parents is paramount to them."

"That's not unusual," Fumahadi said. "It's rare, but there are other sentient species like theirs that reproduce asexually. They are genetically clones; if an offspring isn't like her mother something changed in development, some environmental influence. It would be easy for a species to assume difference meant defect; in their case it usually does."

"Changes in environment," my mother repeated. "The colonists were too few to affect this system much, living on the surface as they did. The corporation was intending to go underwater, but they never really got started."

"The building materials were brought down," I said, checking my notes. "The corporation won't confirm if the drilling for supports had begun. Perhaps it had. Perhaps the drilling brought the Hydridae out of hiding?"

"The corporation won't offer a bit of information it doesn't have to; their evasion here doesn't necessarily mean anything. But something changed; the Hydridae came out of the deep after being invisible to us since the first probe came here more than a century ago," Fumahadi said. "There were signs of structures on the ocean floor, but they had been long since abandoned."

"They gained a food source," Naledi said. "They have similarities to other asexually reproducing species in normal circumstances, but when food is scarce they suddenly breed sexually, the fertilized eggs resting in a spore state until food is again available. That's why the

League scientists called them Hydridae. Once there is food enough to sustain them they hatch and suddenly you have a full population again."

"You theorize," Fumahadi said.

Naledi shrugged, barely perceptible to us from where she lay on the bunk with her hands laced behind her head. "It fits the data."

"If they are first generation, never knew their parents, that could explain their parenting fixation," my mother said. The kettle whistled and she filled the tea pot.

"Also about the absence of Kala," I added. "They said she was 'in bud' but two of the three with us also had young forming off their trunks."

"She must have been further along," Fumahadi said. "Do you suppose they can communicate even before they separate from their mothers?"

"If they could, and if this one didn't show the homogeneity to the mother they expect, that would explain why we would find her state 'confusing'," my mother said.

We stayed up for a few hours more prepping for the opening of negotiations. Fumahadi felt confident from her exchanges with Kala that what the Hydridae really wanted was access to spaceships usable by aquatic creatures. There was a League ally, not member, who had built such things, but the Tritons were notoriously hard to negotiate with. It seemed likely the colonists would be allowed to return but we weren't sure what the corporation would do about their mining station. As always Fumahadi would make clear that they were a separate entity and she did not speak for or even to them.

At some point in the night, whether minutes or hours after I shut my eyes I don't know, a small shaking of the bunk roused me. Naledi dropped catlike to the floor. I watched her cross the room, sleepily wondering why she was taking her bag with her to the bathroom, then saw she was heading out the door, back into the dark conference room.

I sat up, looking at the bunk where my mother and Fumahadi slept. Nighttime wandering was one of the things I remembered about Naledi, and it probably meant nothing but her usual restless curiosity. I had never gone with her and the other children of diplomats who inevitably followed her on these secret excursions. I had always been so serious. Now that I had passed my exams and achieved my goal of early entry into apprenticeship, I wished I had explored more and studied less. And in that moment I wanted to see what adventure Naledi was up to.

I crept up to the doorway but stopped in the shadows and watched as she pulled footies and gloves out of her bag then a tight head covering with a clear face plate from brow to chin. They all adhered to her white jumpsuit which I suspected was a pressure suit even before she took out a small oxygen tank and fastened it to a port on her stomach. She used a tool to force open the door our food had appeared from and crawled inside. The snap when the door shut behind her seemed incredibly loud.

I tiptoed up to the window, peering into the murk beyond. It was dark, but surely that bright white suit would ghost through the darkness? But of course this wasn't where the food had come from. She had to be in the waldo kitchen.

I turned and hustled back into the prefab house to fetch my own bag then went back into the conference room so as not to disturb the others and sat down on the sandy floor. My hunch had been correct: Naledi was still wearing the translator's bindi cam and every minute of it was being recorded to my tablet.

I missed seeing the kitchen; she was already in a watery tunnel that spiralled deeper and deeper. I doubted this was mere curiousity anymore, it felt too sneaky. If she really was working for a corporate interest she might be covertly gathering intel, but that didn't feel true. I wasn't surprised when she'd given up on being an apprentice, the rules of comportment had chafed her more than they did a personality like mine, but she had never struck me as the mercenary type either. But if not that, what was she up to? I was almost tempted to use the earpiece to ask her what she was doing.

She hadn't eaten the meat. My mind kept coming back to that detail. Not eating an offered food was an action that required an explanation, an apology, from a League diplomat. She wasn't a League diplomat anymore but still it was a grievous breach of protocol.

Naledi reached a branching of tunnels and looked at a map on the inside of her wrist then took the path to the right. At the end of the tunnel was another door she forced with her tool before slipping quickly inside.

A crowd of bouncing pink balls gathered tightly around her in the room beyond, attracted to her or to her light. She swam through them, up to the top of the dome-shaped cave to a grill that sealed off a narrow passage heading straight up to barely perceptible moonlight. She used her tool on the latch and hinges both, throwing the whole grill to the floor. The pink things needed no prompting to make good their escape.

Prison escape? That's what she was doing? But the Hydridae had so extolled the virtues of these things as foodstuff we felt sure they'd be offered as a trade good, and they'd been so tasty we knew they had the potential to be a major new commodity. So this was a heist?

The Hydridae had assured us they had access to a nearly limitless supply, but when that cave was empty Naledi retraced her route, coming back faster than she had gone in. It made sense they only kept what they needed on hand, but I wondered where the rest of the limitless supply was. Further out to sea? Were these little pink balls going to find their way home now?

I saw that Naledi had already reached the kitchen and as much as I wanted to see it, I didn't want to get caught spying on her. I ran back into the room and put my tablet and bag away, curling up on the bunk and pretending to sleep. But Naledi did not go back to bed, merely passed through the room and out the other door.

I sat up and looked at my sleeping mother. Perhaps it was that homogeneity remark, I don't know, but in the split second I had for deciding, I opted to follow Naledi and not protocol.

I'm not sure why I took my bag, I would have been sneakier without it, but Naledi never looked back.

Her shuttle was the same model used by League diplomats if a bit old, so when she lowered the ramp to climb into the front of the craft I knew the hatch for the baggage compartment would unlock at the same time. As soon as she was out of sight within the shuttle I sprinted to the back of the craft, popped open the hatch and climbed inside. The moment I shut the door I heard the lock snap shut.

Naledi fired up the engines and the shuttle lifted gently off the landing pad. I groped around in the dark, feeling my way along the low, long space further forward to where the smaller hatch in the cabin floor would be. I was crawling over some sort of fine netting, a lot of it. I had reached the front but still hadn't found the trapdoor when the hatch behind me opened. I saw the door handle and grabbed it as the luggage hold filled with wind and the shuttle tipped, sending the netting billowing out behind it.

I was never going to be able to open the door at this angle; the best I could do was hold on with both hands as my legs scissored the open air, hoping I wouldn't tire and let go before the shuttle leveled out. Too much reading and studying had given me a round, soft appearance, but under that was more muscle than one might expect. I didn't panic. Below my dangling feet I saw the netting hit the ocean, two fine tethers still attaching it to the shuttle. The net dragged the surface of the water, where thousands of pink balls bounced on the moonlit waves.

Naledi flew in a few low, lazy circles and I hooked a forearm through the handle to better hang on. Then suddenly we were shooting up into the sky and leveling out as a loud whirring noise surrounded me: the net was being retracted. I looked around the space and doubted there'd be room for me as well as all those pink balls. We were flying close enough to level for me to get my feet under me and open the trapdoor.

I slipped quietly into the shuttle cabin. I was in the back under the rear conference table; the kitchen, bath, bunks and flight seats were between me and Naledi at the controls but still I feared she would look back and see me. I shut the door as softly as I could and huddled under the table clutching my bag.

As the shuttle fired to lift us out of the atmosphere I realized just what a jam my curiosity had gotten me into. It seemed very unlikely that Naledi would return after what had just happened. How was I going to get back to my mother?

I sat there miserably pondering my scant options for what felt like an eternity when suddenly Naledi said, "you might as well come sit by me. We're nearly there and you don't want to miss this."

I sat frozen for a moment, unsure if she was talking to someone else

I hadn't seen and if I should stay as I was, but that was silly. I crawled out from under the table and passed to the front of the shuttle, bag hugged tight to my chest.

"Where are we going?" I asked as I slipped into the copilot's seat.

"The middle of nowhere," she said. So it was a secret, like the identity of her employer.

"Why did you steal the Hydridae's food source?" I asked. "You didn't even eat any."

"It's not their normal food source. It's not even native to their world. The change in shipping lanes to accommodate the colony drove these babies too close to the gravity well, and the Hydridae have benefited quite enough from that already."

"So you're rectifying a human mistake?"

"And trying to prevent a bigger consequence of that mistake. If the Hydridae get the ships they're asking for, there will be a slaughter." Then her attention was on her comm panel, pinging and searching the screens for a response, pinging and searching again.

The answer was not another ship's ping, it was a song without words and yet so sorrowful I felt tears filling my eyes.

"What is that?" I asked. The screens were still showing nothing but far off stars.

"It was a hello," Naledi said, then give me a dry smile. "Imagine if she had said something truly sad, your heart would just break, wouldn't it?" She turned to the console and I watched her type I RETURN AS PROMISED. HERE THEY ARE. Then she flipped the switch that opened the back hatch.

There was more singing, a choir of vocalizations interweaving, and yet I knew only one creature was speaking.

"The translators haven't cracked this one yet," Naledi said to me. "But I feel what she means. Do you feel it?"

I closed my eyes and listened. "Thank you. Thank you. So few but thank you." I opened my eyes and looked to Naledi, who nodded.

"I hate to guess how many of her children the Hydridae ate."

I felt a pang of queasiness in my belly. "They're sentient? Those little pink balls?"

"Not at that stage of their development, not yet."

"You should have said." Not even for politeness would any of us have eaten a sentient being, no matter how important the negotiations, and these had not been so terribly important at all.

"If I had, I doubt I would have saved any."

The song continued, I nearly couldn't bear it. I had eaten something that would have one day gone on to be a singer like this. It felt so wrong.

"It's not so bad as all that," Naledi said, seeing the anguish on my face. "Look, she understands the intent of things I type into this console; it comes out as music much simpler than hers but she will work to understand. She's a mother, they do that."

I nodded and typed I AM SO SORRY I ATE ONE OF YOUR CHILDREN. I DID NOT KNOW AND NOW I MOURN THE LOSS.

The song changed, becoming a complex epic that went on for an hour or more. By the end I knew this strange mother's pain, how her kind was doomed to have millions of young at a time, far too many to care for, and her sorrow as she had to leave them alone in the vastness of space, her loneliness as she waited for the strongest, the cleverest, the most adept or just the most lucky to find her again. Most would die, some even eaten by other beings, and that was part of how the universe worked. But she had very nearly lost all of her children, every last one.

"An usual breeding pattern for a sentient being," Naledi said. "They have the longing to raise them all with love, to teach them and help them grow and mature, but they just can't. The Hydridae don't understand them at all. In their eyes, these creatures throw their children out into the universe to let them just tumble up on their own any way they can."

"I can see why even their hello sounds so sad. Every mother losing so many of her babies. Everyone that survives knows she has lost so many sisters. That's a hard life for a feeling creature."

Then Naledi leaned over the console again. TAKE THE LITTLE ONES AND RUN. RUN FAR. RUN DEEP. YOU ARE BEING HUNTED.

The song became two interwoven melodies, one thanking Naledi for her warning and one forgiving me for what I had unknowingly done.

A thousand smaller voices tentatively joined in, their songs tremulous yet lovely, a sad farewell to their rescuer. Then the song faded away and we were alone.

"What do you think?" Naledi asked.

"About what?" I asked, wiping tears from my eyes.

"Well, I see you brought your bag. Are we going onward or back?"

I was surprised by the question. "You want me to travel with you? Be your apprentice?"

Naledi laughed. "I was thinking more like a cohort."

"But I don't even know who you work for."

"Don't you?"

I sat quietly, going over all the events of the day. "You don't work for anybody."

"Just me."

"But the Hydridae said you were sent by someone on our side."

"I made it look that way. And I kept it from Fumahadi's knowledge, which was trickier. But I know the League's communication systems as well as any full-fledged ambassador, and they are very easy to hack."

"So what are you doing next?"

"I don't know yet. I'll find someone else that needs a less formal kind of help than the League provides. Don't you want to come with me?"

I did. I desperately did. But in the end I shook my head.

"I don't think I'm ready. I know I studied hard and aced my exams, but I'm starting to see that that doesn't mean much. I want to help you, but I think I need to spend more time as an apprentice before I can be a... cohort."

"I thought that's what you would say, but I had to try," Naledi said and set the shuttle on a course back to the Hydridae world. "But I'll be around. I'm sure if you change your mind you'll know how to find me."

"If you're in the communication system, then yes," I said.

"Fumahadi had put in to have you as her apprentice, you know."

"No, I didn't know that."

"Your mother had first choice, of course. Fumhadi hasn't had an apprentice since me, has she? I feel bad about that. She was a good teacher, I was just the wrong pupil. She works a lot with your mom, you'll still have lots of opportunities to learn from her. But always watch, always listen. You can learn a lot by what they *aren't* teaching you."

I nodded, not sure exactly what she meant but certain I would with time. "Are they going to be OK now? These... what are they called?"

"I didn't feel it was my place to name them," Naledi said. "The universe is big and full of places to hide. I think they'll be just fine. But I'll be watching the Hydridae, just to be sure."

I settled into the copilot's seat, wondering how the next day's negotiations were going to go. If anyone could smooth this over, Fumahadi could.

And I just might learn something.

DEATH SPIRAL

Sanyah Allani had fallen asleep with the hologram running again. The chair she slouched in might be the same as the one in her quarters, but it was never as cozy there surrounded by rough-hewn rock walls as it was in her virtual reality. The fire in particular was always such a vivid illusion she could almost feel its warmth and smell the seasoned wood slowly turning into ash.

The hologram dropped instantly when the call came through, thrusting her too quickly back into reality. The figure of her husband Desmon on the chair opposite hers looked up at her in surprise, then flickered out of existence, leaving her staring at the rock wall that was much closer to her than his chair had been.

Now she was in her own ever-cold room on the mining asteroid, the one she worked really hard not to think of as a cave. But it felt like a cave. Cold and damp, especially after her years in the controlled environment of a Martian orbiting station. She had run every kind of check there was, but nothing in the environmental systems backed up her sense that she was always smelling something moldy. And she had never been able to follow the scent to find the source either.

But it lingered. It was always there. And she always smelled it most strongly just after her hologram shut down.

She tapped her communicator, more to stop its annoying buzzing than out of a desire to answer the call. She glanced at the nearest screen. It was the middle of the night, as much as that meant anything on an asteroid.

"Allani here," she said and pushed herself out of the chair she had settled too far into. Her joints protested, just like they always did these days, and she started to pace the length of her room to get everything loosened up.

"Allani, we have a situation." It was Isbel Delin, the woman in charge of the human half of the mining asteroid. She sounded even more tired and annoyed than Allani felt, and Allani guessed she had been woken up by a call of her own just a few minutes before.

"Something with the stigmergs?" Allani guessed. She stopped her pacing in front of her mirror and realized she had fallen asleep in her uniform. She brushed her hands down the wrinkles of her uniform pants and lifted the front of her shirt to check the smell. It would do. She reached for her jacket.

"I'm really hoping if we act fast, it won't be," Delin said.

Allani stopped moving, one arm halfway through the sleeve of her jacket. "Your tone is spooking me, Delin."

"Probably because I'm spooked," Delin said. "I'm sending you a location point. Meet me there as quickly as you can."

"Will do," Allani said, but to dead air. Delin had already signed off.

Allani fingercombed her short, steel-gray hair into shape. Then she grabbed her belt from where she always hung it by the door. It had all the tools she needed as the chief of security. Most of those tools were for communication or for the recording and collecting of evidence. But she also had a gun. She was trained in how to use it, but had never once had to draw it. She hoped whatever was going on wasn't going to change that.

But she didn't like the edge of panic she had heard in Delin's voice. Something was very wrong.

And she didn't want the stigmergs to know about it. What did that mean?

Allani hated navigating around the asteroid. She had been living here for months, and it was still an incomprehensible maze to her. Unlike the orderly corridors of a space station, the tunnels through the asteroid went in all possible directions. It was like trying to find your way through the inside of the strands of pasta in a plate of spaghetti. A lot of the times, the tunnels didn't even connect. She had learned that quickly, but still couldn't avoid the constant hassle of finding herself staring at a dead end she thought was leading her somewhere.

At least the first step was easy: taking the elevator from the human habitation area down to the mining levels. But the inside of the elevator car had a faint aroma like someone had washed everything down with undiluted vinegar.

Stigmerg smell. It didn't bother her the way the moldy smell in her quarters did, but it was strong enough to make her eyes water as she stood there, waiting to reach her level. The only reason it would be in this car was if the stigmergs had sent a representative to call on Delin. Which they had a few days before. Allani had been there as chief of security. It had been the fifth time she had been face to face with a stigmerg.

The stigmergs had colonies all over Mars, but she had never interacted with any of them while serving in the orbiting station. She had seen pictures of them before, but seeing a picture of an ant the size of a pony was one thing. Being in the presence of one was altogether different.

There was the smell, of course. It was even stronger when you were in the room with them. Then there was the constant clicking noise, the noise that meant nothing. They didn't communicate through sound. No, to understand their communication, you had to pay very close attention to the gradations in that vinegar smell.

As far as Allani knew, no human could do it. Some could tell strong emotions like anger or panic, but the thoughts inside of the stigmergs heads were still a mystery to them.

The stigmergs and some human scientists had developed a machine together that bridged the gap somewhat. But it was far from a perfect solution. Emotions came through far stronger than rational thoughts, which wasn't a great basis for any kind of negotiation.

And this asteroid was a joint mining venture. Which meant that Delin had to work with her stigmerg counterpart. This mostly involved dividing up the territory and leaving each other alone, but shortly after Allani had arrived, something had changed. Something was upsetting the stigmergs, but just what it was wasn't clear.

Except, ironically, they didn't like something they were smelling. And it wasn't Allani's mystery mold. It was something else. The head stigmerg kept coming back to discuss it with Delin, but despite everyone in the room working hard to understand each other, that understanding was too elusive.

The elevator stopped and the doors slid open to show a long, dark mining tunnel. But just to the right of the doors, waiting for her with a glowing light in her hand, was Delin.

"I figured you might get lost again, and time is of the essence," Delin said, her tone completely lacking her usual humor.

"The stigmergs have been complaining about a smell. Have you found where it's coming from?" Allani asked as she jogged to keep up with Delin.

"I hope not," Delin said grimly. "You know they hate that name," she added.

"I know. I've never once said it in front of any of them. But it's awkward only using pronouns. And I can't pronounce a sequence of smells," Allani said. "And they've yet to give us a better name to call them."

"They are as baffled by the idea of a sequence of sounds as we are by the smells," Delin said. "I don't think the original scientists who started calling them stigmergs meant any offense, but I can kind of see why they'd take it that way."

"If they want us to have more joint ventures with them like this place, they're going to need to come up with something," Allani grumbled. "Do you know what they call us?"

Delin gave her a tight grin. "I imagine it's no more flattering than our name for them. Maybe it's best we don't know." Then she nodded towards the mouth of a narrower tunnel they were approaching. "It's just in there."

"Great," Allani said, mostly to herself.

Another thing that life on a space station had never forced upon her: crawling on her hands and knees through a tight space between rocks that always developed sharp protrusions just were she was setting down her weight.

Luckily, this tunnel was only narrow for a few meters. Then they were in a womb-like space, the walls all rounded smooth like the inside of a cocoon.

But the thing curled up in the center of the space was no caterpillar.

It was a human. And even as it lay there with its back to the two of them climbing in through the opening, Allani could tell it was a man.

"Shit," she said, stumbling in her crawl and landing hard on one hip. She could smell dead flesh, just barely. Decomposition hadn't set in yet, but it was close.

There was another smell too, a smell Allani would be sure she was imagining except it was so strong. Crusty bread.

Allani pressed a hand to her forehead, willing the smell to pass. Smelling bread, wasn't that a sign of a stroke?

"You see the problem," Delin said, misreading Allani's reaction. "We have to get rid of this before the stigmergs find out."

"What if they already know?" Allani asked. "If they think we're hiding something from them, it will be worse than if we just admitted what we found here."

"We're far from their territory. I don't think they know," Delin said.

"Who found it?" Allani asked.

Delin barked out a humorless laugh. "One of the support crew got lost bringing repair parts to the main drill," she said. "She came straight to me personally. Smart kid. This is pretty far from everything. I think we'll be okay."

Allani said nothing. She crawled closer to the body using just her knees, pulling on gloves as she went. She touched the body gently on the shoulder, almost as if she were afraid of waking him up. But the body was cold and stiff under her hand. He had been dead alone here for quite some time.

"Someone knows he's here," Allani said. "Someone has to. Someone sneaked him in."

"I don't think we'll be able to keep it secret for long," Delin said.

"Just long enough to have answers before the stigmergs come demanding them."

"Do you think this is what they were complaining about smelling?" Allani asked. She rolled the body onto its back. It was a young man, maybe mid-twenties, with scraggly dark hair and the beginnings of an unkempt beard. His clothes were covered in the dust that coated every tunnel throughout the asteroid. He looked like he had been crawling around inside the asteroid for a week or two anyway. Not longer than that, unless he'd originally been shaving.

"That was my first thought as well," Delin said.

"And?"

"They were so specific about it when we established this place," she said, her eyes unfocused as if she were gazing back through time to that first meeting. "No males. Not even infants. Only women can work the human side. Because male humans release a pheromone that they cannot tolerate."

"Can't tolerate how?" Allani asked.

"It disrupts their ability to communicate with each other?" Delin said with a shrug. "It was never totally clear. The scientists who facilitated that meeting had better equipment than the machine I have in my office, but not much better. But their emotions were strong, and there was no arguing with that. No men on the human side, ever."

"So where did this one come from?" Allani mused to herself.

"That's what I need you to find out, as soon as you can," Delin said. "I can disappear a body, but like you said, someone already knows. Someone helped him get here. I need to be absolutely sure he's the only one."

"I'm on it," Allani said.

Three days later the body had been shipped to Ceres for identification, and the stigmergs seemed none the wiser. But they were still complaining about whatever it was that they smelled.

And Allani was no closer to answers to any of it.

She and her meager team had reviewed every bit of video from every angle of the docking bay, but nothing had gone on or off the asteroid that hadn't had its contents scanned and verified. How ever that man had gotten onto the asteroid, he hadn't been a stowaway. And he hadn't taken the place of any cargo. A thorough inventory had found absolutely nothing missing. Certainly nothing man-sized.

So Allani had circled back to where she had started: the cocoon-like cave far from the active parts of the mine. And the girl who had found him there.

She had assumed when Delin had called her a "smart kid," she had been speaking from that place both she and Allani lived in, the world where they were older than most of the equipment they used and half the stations they dwelt in. To the two of them, most of the inhabitants of the Solar System felt like kids.

But this girl really was a kid. Allani looked from her records displayed on the tablet in her hands up to the girl sitting hunched up small in the chair across the desk from her and then back again.

If anything, she looked older in the photo taken for her records.

"Rosia Kasra," Allani said, both reading the name off the tablet and addressing the girl across from her. Rosia mumbled a response, tucking her body up even smaller as if she wished she could collapse in on herself and disappear. Allani gave her what she hoped was a reassuring smile. "You're not in trouble her, Miss Kasra. I just have a few questions for you."

"Yes, chief," Rosia said miserably.

Allani switched off the tablet and set it down, then folded her hands over it. "Have you been here long?"

"I came on the same ship you did," Rosia said.

"Did you?" Allani said in surprise. "I'm sorry I don't remember you."

"There were five of us," Rosia said. She blushed furiously but still got the words out, "and you were still really sad."

"The word is 'grieving'," Allani said, but she couldn't deny the girl was probably right. Her feelings had still been raw when she'd taken the job rather than retiring alone to the cabin on Earth she and Desmon had saved up their whole lives to buy together. She had sold it before coming here never having seen it.

But she knew what the living room looked like. She knew that very well.

"Chief?" Rosia said, and Allani pulled her mind back to the present.

"I thought I was the only one still getting lost in the tunnels," Allani said to Rosia. "As chief of security, most of my time is spent in the docking bay or in the administrative offices. I don't get down to the mines much. But you work down there, don't you?"

"I'm a fetcher," Rosia said. "I'm not old enough to do actual mine labor yet, but I run and get whatever anyone needs. I don't have a specific team I stick with or anything. I have to go all over."

"I would think that would argue for you knowing the tunnels *better* than others," Allani said.

"I think the other fetchers do," Rosia said, squirming in her chair. "I just can't get it all in my head. It's like… if I could just see it from the outside maybe I'd get it."

"I know what you mean," Allani said with a sigh. "I can't get a mental map in my head either. To be honest, when I'm down there, I usually find someone who looks like they know where they're going, and I just follow them."

"Does that work?" Rosia asked.

"Well, usually when they see me following, they ask me where I'm trying to get to," Allani admitted. "Maybe that doesn't work for you."

"No, I'm supposed to work it out on my own," Rosia said. "I suppose the ants think the same thing."

"What's that?" Allani asked.

"Sorry, stigmergs," Rosia said, as if correcting a faux-pas. Which, given Allani's recent conversation with Delin, was ironic. But slang terms had a way of creating themselves, and some were always more offensive than others. Somehow, Allani didn't think the aliens would like being called "ants" any better than being called "stigmergs."

But that wasn't what she had meant. "What do you mean they think the same thing?" she asked.

"Oh, that if they follow anyone they see, that they'll get to where they're going," Rosia said. "When they get lost in the mines, that's what they do. They find one of us and follow us. The others when they notice a stigmerg behind them just walk them towards their half of the asteroid. Once they get close enough to recognize where they are, they scuttle off. But I feel bad when one gets behind me. I can't lead it anywhere."

"I thought everything was kept separate?" Allani said.

"Up here it is, but down there, it's kind of impossible not to mix," Rosia said. "We don't mine the same places, but our paths still cross all the time. But no one makes in trouble, not on our side or on theirs."

"That's something, I suppose," Allani said, putting a mental pin in that to ask Delin about it later. "So you found this dead body, but he wasn't in a main tunnel or even a walkable one."

Rosia flushed a dark red again. She wasn't squirming in her chair, but she was gripping the arms with whitened fingers as if fighting the impulse.

"You knew he was there," Allani guessed.

"I was lost," Rosia said.

Allani sighed, then switched her tablet back on. "I've checked on some things, Miss Kasra. You weren't scheduled to be on duty on the shift in question. You had been on sleep rotation for a full six hours. Just how lost are you telling me you were?"

"I," Rosia said, but then shut her mouth without saying another word. Her lip trembled and she bit down on it hard enough to draw blood.

Allani stood up to reach across her desk and gently grasp the girl's bony arm. She could feel every muscle in her little body tensed up so tight it just had to hurt.

But at the softest of squeezes from Allani's hand, all the tension rushed out of Rosia's body. She collapsed down into the chair, wrapped her arms around her head, and sobbed.

"Stop it. Pull yourself together. I still have questions for you," Allani snapped. The girl raised her head out of her arms, but her tear-filled eyes were absolutely wounded. Allani focused on a point in the middle of her forehead. Sympathy would have to wait. For all she knew, this girl was the murderer.

Did you kill him?" Allani asked her.

"No," Rosia said. For whatever reason, the question seemed to calm her. She sat up and wiped the tears from her face. "He was dead when I got there."

"With bread," Allani guessed.

"I had a whole basket of food, but I guess I was too late. Not because I got lost, I don't mean that. They sent me too late. They knew right where he was, but they didn't send me for so long I guess he just died waiting," Rosia said.

It was a grim image, but Allani was fairly certain it wasn't a true one. Why would that man just starve to death waiting there for help? Nothing about the body had indicated that he couldn't move on his own.

But it wasn't the most pertinent question. "Rosia, who is this 'they'?" Allani asked.

Rosia was squirming in her chair again, but Allani fixed her with a stern glare and she instantly sat still. "I was brought here from an orphanage on Ceres as part of a youth work program," she said.

"So your record states," Allani said.

"But that isn't sponsored by the mining company. It was set up by the other miners. Did you know that?" Rosia asked.

"I did not," Allani admitted.

"There are six of us here now," Rosia said. "We're hired as fetchers, but that's not what we really do here."

"What do the other miners need children for?" Allani asked. She was musing to herself, but since she had done it out loud, Rosia answered for her.

"We can get through the beehive," she said.

"I'm sorry, what?" Allani asked.

"The beehive," Rosia said. "I might as well just show you. You'll know all about it soon enough. Everyone says so. They're really afraid."

"*Everyone* says?" Allani repeated, rubbing at the bridge of her nose tiredly. "Rosia, just what is going on here?"

"It's not bad," Rosia insisted. "I don't know why that man died, or why he even was where he was, but that was just an accident. Honestly. Please, if you just let me show you. It's not bad, and I don't think once you see it you'll want to even tell the mining company what's going on."

"I work for the mining company," Allani told her. "It's my job to tell them what's going on."

"I'm not going to tell you anything," Rosia said, suddenly stubborn.

"You either see with your own eyes or try to find it yourself. I'm not talking. I'll go back to the orphanage first."

Allani didn't really have any way to coerce the girl to talk. She could fire her, send her back to Ceres. Perhaps that would be the simplest thing. But she wouldn't learn anything that way.

She could get actual law enforcement involved, if she had proof that anything criminal was going on. Which she didn't.

Or she could go see whatever it was that Rosia wanted to show her.

"Then, by all means, show me this beehive," Allani said at last. She sent messages to both of her subordinates about where she was going and what she was doing, and she checked the charge on her gun before leaving her office. Her gut told her all of that was overkill, but sometimes it was better not to listen to your gut.

Rosia led the way down the elevator to the mining levels, even deeper than where the body had been found.

"They can't use the mining equipment to get through the beehive," Rosia said as they headed deeper into the asteroid. "All of that is tracked by the company, right? I mean, people argue with whether the cameras are always running, but the location trackers absolutely are, right?"

"That's what they tell me," Allani said.

"So they can't risk letting them anywhere near the beehive," Rosia said. The elevator had stopped at the lowest level and Rosia took a glowing lantern from a stack of them by the door and led the way down a winding tunnel. It was tall enough to walk through, but far too narrow for any of the mining equipment.

Allani had a sudden horrid thought. "Please tell me we're not in the stigmerg part of the mine," she hissed at Rosia.

"No, they're not here," Rosia assured her. "And the tunnel we're taking will take us even further from their territory. That was on purpose."

"On purpose by whom?" Allani asked. "Just how many of the miners are part of this thing? I can't imagine funding youth work programs is cheap."

"Everyone contributes to that fund, even the ones who aren't part of it," Rosia said.

"Part of what?" Allani demanded. She was losing patience with having her questions danced around.

She was also losing her wind more than she'd like to admit. After taking the elevator all the way down to the center of the asteroid, the tunnel they were trekking up now felt like it was taking them all the way back to the surface at the steepest angle that could still be walked. Allani already felt the beginnings of a stab in her diaphragm.

"I'm sorry. But I really had to take you the long way," Rosia said, slowing her pace until Allani caught up.

"Why?" Allani said.

"The miners in charge aren't going to like it that I'm showing you this," Rosia said. "But whether you find out on your own or I show you, either way I just know I'm getting dumped back into the orphanage on Ceres. This way maybe you'll find me another job in the mining company, even though I'm technically still underage."

"No promises," Allani said, but Rosia motioned for her to be silent. She listened intently at nothing Allani could hear, then started up the slope again at a creeping pace.

Allani drew her weapon before following.

But then she heard the last sound she ever expected to her within the tunnels of the asteroid mine.

She heard a baby's cry.

"Rosia?" Allani asked, but the girl didn't look back. She just quickened her steps up the slope then around a bend in the tunnel.

Allani ran after her, but when she reached the bend in the tunnel, there was no longer any sign of Rosia. But there were more voices ahead. The baby crying, women arguing, Rosia arguing back.

And men. Allani distinctly heard the voices of men.

She brandished her firearm as she sprinted up the last stretch of the narrow tunnel into a larger, mining machine-sized tunnel.

But that tunnel was complete chaos. People were running everywhere, and children were crying. Several women ran straight at Allani, waving their arms as if desperately hoping to obscure her view.

But Allani saw clearly enough. Men were fleeing in all directions, some on their own, others with children in their arms. And the floor was littered with overturned cots and strewn blankets. Plastic crates were everywhere, filled with clothes or food or tablets and games.

Allani raised her weapon, and the women who had been rushing at her all pulled back. But they didn't flee.

"What is this?" Allani demanded.

The one directly in front of her, a heavy-set woman of about thirty with a drill-operator's goggles dangling around her neck, lifted her chin in defiance. Then she said, "our families."

"I told you it wasn't bad," Rosia said, her voice almost a wail.

"We weren't hurting anybody," the drill operator said. "But one week back on Ceres every six months? That's not human. We have families."

"Families you were absolutely not allowed to have here," Allani growled. "That was a term of your employment here. You agreed to it."

"It's not human," the drill operator said again.

Allani just tapped on her communicator and patched herself into the public address system. "General alert! All hands to the tunnels. Get every man to the docking bay. Now!"

Her voice rose loud enough on that last word to create a shriek of feedback from the speakers somewhere over her head through her wrist communicator, but she felt that only stressed her point.

"You have no idea what you've done," Allani said to the drill operator.

"I know the stigmergs will only work with female humans," the drill operator said, crossing her arms and giving Allani a smug look. Like being taller made her more right.

"Did you think that was a political preference?" Allani growled back.

"Isn't it?" Still that smug look.

"We have no idea why they won't allow male humans on this aster-oid. We only know they feel very strongly about it," Allani said. "Very, very strongly."

Something wavered in the drill-operator's eyes. "Are you saying our men are in danger?"

"It's a possibility," Allani said. "Find your men. Get them to the docking bay and off this asteroid. Now."

The few women who still lingered in the cave there with Allani promptly scattered through the tunnels. Allani really hoped they all had a plan for where to meet their families worked out in advance. That they knew where to find them now.

"They really were smelling something," she said to herself, putting her gun away and kicking a twisted blanket out of her way. "Stowaways."

"Not stowaways," Rosia said. Allani hadn't realized she was still there. She was holding an armful of clothing and dumped it into one of the crates then bent to set an overturned cot back on its feet.

"How did they get here?" Allani asked.

"There's a cave on the surface and a tunnel mouth that's pretty close to it," Rosia said. "Ships can be bribed to bring families here to the cave. They have to run over the surface to the tunnel mouth to get to here. It's tricky timing with the orbiting security cameras, especially for the ships, and the families have to run over the surface in pressure suits."

"And that dead man in the tunnel was the first accident?" Allani said, shaking her head. It was almost unbelievable, how much had to go the miners' way for this all to be possible. "So this cave is the beehive?"

"No, the beehive is the system of really small tunnels that lead from here to the back of the cave itself. Too small for grown people, but big enough for us fetchers to get through. We bring in the supplies that way. No one has ever stolen anything from the mining corporation. Not so much as a slice of bread," Rosia said.

"No, the rules you were breaking were quite a bit bigger than theft," Allani said. "How many men were down here?"

But before Rosia could answer, Allani's communicator started buzzing.

"Allani here," she said.

"It's Delin. We have a situation," she said.

"I'm on it," Allani said. "Although calling for all hands might've been overkill. I think the women down here are tracking down their own families. We should have everything locked down soon enough."

"It's too late," Delin said, and there was a hitch to her voice.

"The stigmergs know?" Allani guessed. "Are they complaining already?"

"Worse," Delin said. "I don't know what they're doing, but it's definitely worse. I need you in the main cavern now."

The main cavern was the heart of the mine, where the stigmerg territory and the human territory met. No one lingered in that area, but everyone knew how to find it. Including Allani.

Then tunnel she and Rosia took to get there opened up on a ledge far above the cavern floor. Not where Allani had expected to be, but it was quickly apparent that that was probably a good thing.

"What are they doing?" Rosia asked, catching hold of Allani's hand and squeezing it tightly.

"I have no idea," Allani admitted. But it didn't look good.

No, it looked like every stigmerg on the asteroid, every miner and every support worker and whatever other administrative distinctions their species had, every one of them had come here to the cavern in the center of everything.

And once here, they had just started moving in circles. Even as Allani and Rosia looked down on it, she could see they were moving faster and faster. The clicking sound was echoing all around them, and the vinegar smell was chokingly pungent.

Allani looked up from the milling aliens long enough to find Delin standing helplessly off to one side. Then, Rosia in hand, Allani found a way down to the main floor then skirted close to the wall until she had reached Delin's side.

"What are they doing?" Allani asked. She had to shout to be heard over the clicking and the clatter of exoskeleton feet over stone.

"I don't know," Delin said.

"I guess they were right about not allowing men here?" Allani suggested.

"I have people on the docking bay counting heads as we load up the shuttles," Delin said.

"You know how many men were here?" Allani asked.

"The first wave to reach the docking bay after your announcement included a woman who had a list," Delin said. "I hope her list is right."

Allani said nothing, but when Rosia clung more tightly to her side, she just put an arm around the girl and hugged her close.

Hours ticked by. All of the men and children were accounted for and sent back to Ceres. Allani had arranged with the security forces there to take over, holding everyone until they knew whether the mining company was going to press charges. That part of things was out of Allani's hands.

But even after they had confirmed twice that every man was gone, the stigmergs just kept racing around in circles. Ever faster circles. And the vinegar stink grew.

"They are in distress, I think," Delin said. "I've contacted everyone with any knowledge of the stigmergs, but no one has ever seen anything like this."

"No one knows how to stop it?" Allani guessed.

"No one," Delin said.

"They look so sad," Rosia said. She hadn't left Allani's side since this had all started. Allani guessed she was still hoping that Allani could help her not go back to that orphanage. Allani had no idea what she could do for Rosia. She hadn't had time to even give it any thought yet.

"You're anthropomorphizing," Delin said dismissively.

"Is she? We know they're think creatures," Allani said.

"We have no clue how or what they think," Delin said.

Allani said nothing. She supposed that was true.

"Anyway, I think they all look lost," Rosia said.

Allani watched the stigmergs as they raced by. They were tiring, she could tell. They were starting to stumble and fall into each other. Soon one would fall to the ground, and the others would surely trample right over it.

Would that hurt a stigmerg? They had exoskeletons, after all.

But another thought suddenly exploded in her mind. "Rosia's right. They look lost," she said. She turned to give Delin a look that Delin clearly didn't understand.

"What are you saying?" Delin asked.

"I'm saying they're lost," Allani said, gesturing towards the tornado of stigmergs. "The scent of our men messed up their sense of... I don't know. Everything. And now they're stuck here. They don't know how to get out of this."

"So what can we do about it?" Delin asked, impatient.

But Rosia had figured out what Allani was thinking already. She looked up at both of them, her face bright. "We can lead them out!"

"How?" Delin asked.

"The miners do it all the time, apparently," Allani said. "When a lone stigmerg gets too far from the others, they find a human and follow her. It happens so often the miners all know when there's a stigmerg following you around, you just walk towards their side of the asteroid."

"Then they recognize where they are and scuttle away," Rosia said.

"Probably more by scent than by sight, but the end result is the same," Allani said.

"I can't ask a miner to go out into that mass of stigmergs," Delin said.

"Not one. It's going to take all of us," Allani said. "All of our scent."

Another call was put out for all hands to gather in the main cavern. The collection of miners who turned up were all clearly wrestling with big emotions. No one had yet said a word about what disciplinary action would be taken, and Allani guessed more than a few of them were bracing for the worst. It took Delin a few tries to get them to focus their attention on her and not the question of when they would see their families again.

But just their presence there was having an effect on the spiral of racing stigmergs. Their tight formation was loosening, forming something like a bulge of more widely spaced runners on the edge closest to where Delin had assembled all the miners.

"None of them are peeling away yet," Allani mumbled to herself. "Maybe this won't work."

"It will work," Rosia said. "Watch."

She waved her arms as if that would draw any stigmerg attention, then she turned and ran down the sloping corridor that led to the nonhuman side of the asteroid.

Delin was still yelling instructions, but the miners who saw Rosia running quickly realized what was happening and immediately started running after her.

Then a few of the stigmergs broke away from the others. Just a handful, but it was a start. More of the miners got the idea and started running, and more of the stigmergs followed.

"Come back for more once you lose your tails!" Allani shouted into her communicator. Her voice echoed through the mine speakers even as she started running herself.

Less than an hour later, not a living stigmerg remained in the cavern. But a dozen or so were collapsed on the ground, dead from exhaustion.

"This is going to be a nightmare," Delin said. "It might be the end of this joint venture."

All the human women went back to their quarters. There was no point in mining when you didn't even know if your job still existed, but beyond that they were all exhausted from all the running.

Allani tracked down the drill-operator. Her name was Talla Drak, and while she denied being in charge of anything, she was clearly one of the leaders.

"Are we all fired?" Drak asked.

"Not a clue," Allani said. "If it's any comfort, if you're fired then I'm fired. And I didn't even do anything."

"How is that a comfort?" Drak asked.

Fair point. Allani got down to what might be the last bit of business before she was unemployed.

"Who was the man we found dead?" Allani asked.

"Him?" Drak said. "He doesn't matter."

"Indulge me," Allani said, putting just enough edge to her voice to get through even to this obstinate woman.

"His name was Vaek Darrow," she said. "He's the husband of Rolla Darrow, one of the other drill-operators."

"Why wasn't he in the cave with the others?" Allani asked.

"He hit Rolla," Drak said. "We don't allow that here. He would've been gone on the next ship, but the ship was delayed. Apparently you changed up the orbits of the security cameras. It took a few days before it was safe to schedule another delivery."

Allani had done no such thing, but one of her subordinates probably had. It was good security protocol, and as much as Allani was new on the mining asteroid, her employees had been there for years.

"So Rosia was right," Allani said. "You put him in a cave and forgot about him?"

Drak just shrugged. "We intended to feed him. But the schedule we had drawn up didn't get updated when the ship was delayed. So. We all work long hours, you know."

"Yeah, you did," Allani said, and left in disgust.

The next day, five ships full of mining company executives arrived. Allani guessed that half of them were lawyers, and that no one was going anywhere until they had a complete picture of what had happened, who was to blame, and how they could spin all this with the stigmergs.

No one had seen the stigmergs in the mines, but Rosia had sneaked over to their network of caves and reported back that they all appeared to be sleeping but not dead.

Then, to Allani's surprise, she was summoned to Delin's office less than an hour after the executives' arrival. And Delin wasn't there. Some other woman was using her desk with an air that said it was hers now.

"I'm guessing I'm fired," Allani said as she sat down. "Are you telling us all individually?"

"I assure you, you're not fired," the woman said. "Actually, I'm here to talk to you about a transfer. We have a Martian outpost that is having difficulties with their stigmerg neighbors. Things are getting out of hand, and we could really use your expertise. Are you interested? There would, of course, be a pay increase."

Allani opened her mouth to object to the idea she was an expert in anything, then she shut it again.

She opened it to question why her fumbling of this particular matter would lead to a pay increase, but then closed it again.

The third time she opened her mouth, she said, "I would need to bring my assistant with me."

"Sure, of course," the woman said. "Whatever you need."

"She's here as part of a youth work program set up with an

orphanage on Ceres," Allani said. "I guess that's going to be a little bit more paperwork taking her to Mars."

"Nothing our lawyers can't handle," the woman said. "But it's imperative we get you to Mars right away."

"Then I'll go fetch my assistant and meet whoever on the hangar bay," Allani said.

She had no idea what she was about to face, but one thing she was sure of. There was no way Rosia was going to say no to the opportunity.

WHILE THE RAT'S AWAY

The last thing I remembered before the drugs took me was the smell of the antiseptic that had been sprayed inside the cold sleep mask before it had been placed over my face. It had been distinctly unpleasant, like a metallic kind of minty smell that was far too strong. It made me more than a little suspicious. It was too much like the other places I had passed through since leaving the commune on Mars. In the commune, we had scrubbed diligently and daily. I knew what clean smelled like.

This? Was the overpowering aroma that resulted from someone not wanting you to know just how unclean they were letting things stay. Because spraying a smell was so much easier than scrubbing and sterilizing.

I had only gotten a single whiff of it before the cold sleep had washed over me, though. Not even time to form all those thoughts. No, those thoughts percolated up in my mind as I floated in some liminal space between sleep and wakefulness. In that place, I had nothing to do but smell that smell, and gag on it, and finally to realize with that mask still fitted over my nose and mouth, I really had better not throw up.

Then all at once it was gone, and I sucked in a deep lungful of nonminty air.

"Easy," said a voice I recognized at once as Brother August.

"That was terrible," I said, and heard my voice rasping hoarsely. I wiped my mouth, where drool had dried in sticky, crusty patches, and then at something all too similar that had formed on my eyelids.

Then I took a look around. "This is the place?" I tried not to sound as disappointed as I felt. I knew the new commune was going to be rudimentary, but this was nothing more than bare metallic walls with stacks of supplies yet to even be unpacked. And no windows? Even on Mars, we had had windows. Was the atmosphere on this new world really that bad?

"No, we're awake too soon," Brother August told me.

"In the spaceport?" I guessed. Although the scale felt wrong for that. If anything, I would think we were still on the ship that was taking us across the stars. Not that I had ever seen it. We had been put into cold sleep while still at the clinic on Mars, nowhere near the spaceport that orbited Earth where we were meant to pick up our ride.

It was all very confusing.

"Something's happened, but I don't know what," Brother August said. "Are you doing all right? I need to check on the others."

"Of course. I'm fine," I said, although I desperately wanted a drink of water. But if the others were still suffering in that cloud of metallic mint smell, I could wait.

Suddenly a man nearly as wide as he was tall—and he stood head and shoulders over even Brother August—lumbered into my view. He looked around, his nut-brown hair all standing on end as if channeling his ample nervous energy. His dark eyes skipped over me as if I weren't even there, then fixed on something behind me and to my left. I just scrambled out of his way before he seized on the crate that had been at my elbow. He hugged it to his chest possessively, like a toddler holding his most prized possession, then scuttled away with it, disappearing through a doorway that promptly closed behind him.

It was the sort of door I was familiar with, even with the same high threshold that had to be stepped over. In the commune, those were meant to keep the Martian dust out of the buildings. They almost completely failed at their task. But I really couldn't imagine why anyone would have one inside of a spaceship. Wasn't this supposed to be a sterile space? Or at least dust-free?

But what did I know? This was my first time off the commune. And I wasn't even supposed to be awake to see any of this.

I had just gotten up to take a closer look at the only other door—this door was definitely not like anything I had seen before, and I only guessed it was a door because it was door-shaped and door-height—when I heard Brother August calling for me urgently.

"Sister June! Come here!" he said.

I climbed over a scattered pile of packing crates, wondering in passing if they had been put on the ship in this sort of disarray or if the motion of flying through the stars had somehow sent them tumbling back down from neat stacks. Then I was at Brother August's side. I saw all the other members of our traveling family were awake now. Brothers October and January were helping Brother August shift the heavy lid off what had to be the largest of the boxes. Sister April had found a crate of water bulbs and handed one of them to me with one hand as she sucked thirstily from the bulb she clutched in the other. Sister May had dribbled a little of the water from her own bulb onto a handkerchief and was scrubbing at her face so vigorously her skin was pink.

"Sister June, fetch Kolya," Brother August said, barely even looking back over his shoulder at me before returning his attention to whatever was in the box in front of him.

"Brother… Kolya?" I said, puzzled. "You mean the man who was just here?"

"Kolya, yes," Brother August said, not quite impatiently. "He's our escort. He needs to see this."

"Of course," I said, and climbed back over the spill of crates to the normal-looking door. I had just closed my hand over the opening mechanism when it was ripped from my grasp.

"Brother Kolya?" I said as he stepped over the threshold.

"Just Kolya," he said, then slammed the door shut behind him as if that gesture punctuated his sentence.

"Kolya, yes," I stammered, and I could see his impatience growing.

I gestured to the far end of the—storage room, was it?—where the heads of the others were just barely visible. "Brother August has something to show you."

"Delightful," Kolya said in a way that made it very clear that nothing about this situation was bringing him any delight, me least of all. Then he pushed past me to cross the room, pausing briefly when a crate caught his eye. He carefully extracted it from the spill and set it aside before climbing to where the others waited.

I didn't hear what Brother August said to him, but when I finally found a perch on a stack of crates that had survived intact, I could finally see what had everyone in an uproar.

There, in the heart of the largest box, were a pair of young people. They were curled up together, hugging each other as if for warmth, although the room we were in was quite comfortable in temperature. They reminded me of a story I had read as a little girl, about two children—babes?—lost in the woods. Only these two weren't covered in a blanket of leaves gathered by various woodland creatures.

Also, the children in the story hadn't been clutching badly fogged masks to their own faces.

"Well, that explains that," Kolya said. Although I had no idea what had just been explained.

"Are they all right?" I asked.

"They are sleeping," Brother August assured me. "Cold sleeping, I believe?" He looked to Kolya for confirmation.

"They're stowaways, is what they are," he groused. Then he bent over laboriously, nearly tumbling into the crate himself as he reached to pluck off each of their masks. He ignored Brother August's offer of a hand as he straightened back up even more laboriously than he had leaned over. He turned away from the box, examining the masks in his hands.

"Built these themselves?" he scoffed. "Still, worked well enough. They sapped off enough of our juice to pull us all out of sleep."

"So we're *not* meant to be awake yet," Brother August surmised.

"Of course not," Kolya snapped. "Does this look like your lovely new home?"

"No," Brother August said, unbothered by Kolya's bad temper. "But

I wasn't woken until we'd reached the homestead the last time. I thought perhaps we were in the spaceport on the other side."

Kolya glanced around the room as if reminding himself of what it looked like, which definitely wasn't a spaceport.

"Look, you can see where they sent a crawler drone out of their crate to connect their... masks," he said disdainfully, as if he wanted a different word for what he was holding in his hands but didn't want to bother finding one, "to our cold sleep system. They overloaded it."

"So we can't go back into cold sleep?" Brother August asked calmly.

"No," Kolya said, irritated. "It's shot. I don't have what it takes to bring it back online, and even if I did, there isn't enough juice to get us all back under. We're taking the long road this time."

"Ah, yes. The long road," Brother August said, nodding sagely. Then he glanced at the rest of us. "That is a slang term some escorts use for traveling across the stars outside of cold sleep."

"Yeah, because it takes longer," Kolya said sardonically.

"But we'll still get there?" Sister May asked anxiously.

"Of course we will," Brother August said.

"We have air," I said. "And water. Is there food?"

"There's liquid ration," Kolya said. "Everything a body needs to stay alive, in liquid form for the most accurate measurement. That last bit is going to be important. We have a long way to go, and not a milliliter to waste."

"How long is the long road?" Sister May asked. Her hands were twisting together in her lap.

"I haven't calculated it yet," Kolya admitted gruffly. "I'm still situating things in the... command room. Which is off limits to the rest of you."

"You need have no worries about us, Mr. Kolya," Brother August said. "We will obey your rules, and gladly."

"Just Kolya," he said again. But he was softening now, some of his angry demeanor evaporating away.

But then we all heard a yawn, a long, loud, almost theatrical sound. We turned our attention back to the box to see the stowaways sitting up and wiping at their mouths and eyes. They were both young, barely more than teenagers, although with the over-sized coats they were wearing they looked younger still. Like kids wearing an older siblings hand-me-downs. But they were two of the oddest people I had ever seen, even compared to all the odd people I had seen on my way from the commune to the cold sleep clinic back on Mars.

Their eyebrows were odd, for one. It was like they had shaved away their natural hair and drawn in their own jagged patterns where eyebrows should be, but the shapes were all wrong.

And they both had metallic implants all over their faces, curving around their eyes or over their ears or set just at the corners of their mouths.

They had the same hairstyle, untidy tall masses of it on top, but shaved all around to leave clear space for all that hardware, I supposed.

But one's hair was indigo, and the other's was magenta. That was the only difference I could see between them.

"Street rats," Kolya said disdainfully. Then he shook the masks in his hand at them. "You built these?"

"Sure, we're street rats," the indigo-haired one said with another exaggerated yawn. "You the cat?"

"I am as far as you're concerned," Kolya spat back.

"Mr. Spectre," said the magenta-haired one to the one with indigo hair. "I'm thirsty."

"Oh, here," Sister April said, and gave them each a bulb of water.

"Now, just hold on here," Kolya said, but the two of them sucked down the contents in a startling short period of time.

"Thanks, love," said Mr. Spectre. Then, to his companion, he said, "thank the nice lady, Ms. Ardala."

"I was going to," Ms. Ardala pouted, but morphed her face to a warm smile in an eye blink as she turned to Sister April. "Thank you, love."

"It's Sister April," Sister April stammered, blushing. "Are you still thirsty? We have more."

"Now, just hold on!" Kolya boomed. "Stop feeding the rats."

"They're human beings, Mr. Kolya," Brother August said, gently but firmly.

"They are the reason we aren't happily in cold sleep right now," Kolya said. "I explained about the liquid rations, didn't I?"

"Yes, you did. But surely there's enough for all of us," Brother August said. "There are only two more of us."

"For months, maybe years," Kolya said.

"But you're going to figure out how long soon, right?" I put in.

"Of course," he sputtered. "My point is, we shouldn't be sharing in the first place. These two don't belong here. We're within our rights to space them both and be done with them."

"Space them?" Sister April said uncertainly.

"He means to push them out the airlock and kill them," Brother August said. His tone was still measured, but his habitual gentleness was gone now. "We'll be having none of that, Mr. Kolya."

"I told you, it's just Kolya," he sighed. "Look, I'll do the math and tell you how long this all will last. And I'll measure out everyone's daily ration of liquid nutrient. Every *paying* passenger's daily ration," he clarified. "What you choose to do with it from there is your own business. But I won't be feeding these two. That's not how I run my business."

"I'm sure that's quite satisfactory, Kolya," Brother August said. "There are six of us paying passengers. Stretching our rations out to cover for eight won't be too much of a hardship, I shouldn't think. Nothing like one of our holy fasts, I shouldn't think."

"No, brother!" we all said together.

"Well, cheers, all of you," Mr. Spectre said cheerily. "So, when's that ration coming? I'm so hungry I could eat a rat, since someone brought it up."

"Rations will be distributed at dinnertime," Kolya said. Then, without even explaining what dinnertime was on this ship, he stormed out of the room, stopping on the way to retrieve the crate he had set aside before.

"We have enough for everyone, don't we, Brother August?" Sister May asked.

"Of course we do, Sister," he said. "These things happen. It's part of the contract we signed before beginning this journey. Mr. Kolya swore he would bring enough to keep us alive through the whole journey, if it came to that. And the whole journey would take years and years. So you see, you don't need to worry. Everything will be fine."

Mr. Spectre said something like, "heh." Just a burst of air that exploded out of him. But when we all looked to him to explain, he just shrugged and sucked down the last of his second bulb of water.

Kolya emerged from the room about an hour later to tell us our journey down the long road was going to take five months, two weeks and a day. Then he went back into his room and closed the door.

"There, you see?" Brother August said. "Plenty for us to share, even with our two new companions. Now, let's see about a work rotation. Sister April, will you assist me?"

There was a sudden bustle of motion, as if knowing the length of our journey down to the day somehow had freed all of us to even stand up and walk around. Brothers October and January set themselves to arranging the crates in neat stacks against the walls, and Sister May took the rest of the water bulbs to arrange a kitchen area in one corner. With Brother August and Sister April drawing up a work rotation together, only I was left at loose ends.

I knew I was supposed to be finding something useful to do, like the others were, and I really shouldn't wait until one of the others found a task for me, but I was curious about the stowaways.

For their part, they seemed curious about me as well, and waved me over to sit with them on the edge of their massive crate. I noticed for the first time that the crate they had been hiding in was nothing like the rest of the crates that held all of our supplies for the new homestead. So they hadn't hidden among our baggage themselves. They had sealed themselves up in a box and… what? Hoped for the best?

"What's your name?" Ms. Ardala asked me between tiny sips of her water bulb.

"I'm Sister June," I said, and tried not to blush. I wasn't used to talking to people who weren't part of our commune, but at least these two were less blustery than that Kolya fellow.

"Sister June, and Brother whatsit," Mr. Spectre said. "You're not really siblings, are you? Because that one over there is darker than the black of space, while that one is paler than… well, me."

"Not that we're judging," Ms. Ardala hastened to add.

"Not a bit," Mr. Spectre heartily agreed.

"No, we're not genetic family," I said, then took a deep breath before going on. "We're family within the Church of the—"

"Yes, right," Ms. Ardala interrupted me, but smiled warmly to show there were no bad feelings. "I thought it might be that. Please, say no more."

"No, I wouldn't, of course," I mumbled. My first great chance at witnessing, and I had blown it before even properly getting started.

"Not that we mind," Mr. Spectre said.

"Not a bit," Ms. Ardala agreed.

"So you're all missionaries?" Mr. Spectre asked and sipped at his water bulb.

"Not exactly," I admitted. "Our communes on Mars are getting very crowded, so we're going to found new ones across the stars."

"How romantic," Ms. Ardala said. I honestly couldn't tell if she was being sarcastic or not. I thought she was. But her voice was so warm and friendly.

"Yes, well, Brother August has been there before, and he's seen the aliens who dwell there," I said. "He didn't exactly explain, but he did tell us that they aren't the sort of creature we can spread our message to."

"Not the religious sort?" Mr. Spectre asked.

"More like, they can't hear us speak or notice us if we try to sign to them or something," I said. "I don't really understand it."

"Don't give it a moment's worry," Ms. Ardala assured me. "I'm sure it will all be clear when we arrive."

"Are you coming to the commune with us?" I asked, excited despite myself. I had known my other five traveling companions my entire life. The idea of getting to know someone new was quite novel. "Is that why you stowed away? To join us?"

"Not quite, love," Mr. Spectre said with a look of sorrow I didn't quite understand.

"We were just looking for an adventure, Sister," Ms. Ardala said. "Didn't matter where. We just wanted to be moving."

"We'll probably keep moving," Mr. Spectre said.

"Well, not for the next six months," Ms. Ardala reminded him.

"Love, please," he said with an eye roll. "We're literally moving faster now than we've ever done in our lives."

"That's true," Ms. Ardala agreed, then sucked down the last of her water bulb.

Sometime later, Kolya emerged from the door with a tray of plastic cups, each containing a very paltry amount of some sort of sparkling liquid that was too gel-like to be just water.

"This is it?" Brother August asked, taking one of the cups. "An entire day's worth of ration?"

"Everything a body needs to survive," Kolya said irritably.

"There are only six cups," Brother August pointed out.

"I told you I'm not feeding the rats," Kolya said, then grumbled something else under his breath, something about the airlock.

"Surely we can have two more empty cups, so that we may share as we choose to?" Brother August pressed.

Kolya growled in annoyance, gesturing with the now-empty tray as he disappeared back into the command room. But he re-emerged a moment later with an entire sleeve of plastic cups, still in their sterile packaging. "Knock yourselves out," he said as he thrust the cups at Brother August.

We all gathered around as Brother August lined up the six liquid-containing cups at eye-level on a stack of crates, add two more empties, then poured from one to the other until they all appeared to be the exact same height.

It was less than a swallow, and while the sweet, lemony taste was quite pleasant, it faded from my tongue all too soon.

"We have some things to fix, I should think, Mr. Spectre," Ms. Ardala said when she had downed her share of the ration.

"Indeed, I do agree, Ms. Ardala," Mr. Spectre said. "But for now, we should thank our hosts."

"Verbally for now," Ms. Ardala said.

Then, speaking as one, they thanked us all profusely.

With the day's food consumed, there was nothing more to do. We all curled up on our makeshift beds, and Brother August found the control to dim the lights.

I didn't think I'd ever be able to sleep in such a strange place, so devoid of sounds besides the soft breathing of my companions. Sleeping on the commune meant the constant hum of machines and the soft hiss of the air outside the walls of the dome. This was too quiet. But I was just trying to work out how many more nights I would spend like this—when Kolya said six months, which six months had he meant? Months of thirty days or more or less? Why not just tell us the whole thing in days or at least weeks and days—when I finally drifted off to sleep.

I think it was the math that did it.

The next day, we started our work rotation. Not having any need for a breakfast or lunchtime on the schedule, our morning prayers ran uninterrupted until the early afternoon. Then there were six distinct jobs that Brother August and Sister April had defined for all of us. Every day would be a different job for six days, with a seventh day for rest before starting the rotation all over again.

My job on the first day was sorting the hardware. After prayers had ended, I had opened the crate that Brother August had provided for me, and dumped the contents of every box inside into a large tray. Then I had jostled the tray to mix everything together really thoroughly before sitting down to separate nut from bolt from screw from nail, sorting them all into distinct boxes.

I was contently going about my business for some time before I realized that Ms. Ardala was sitting cross-legged beside me, watching me work.

"You *do* realize this is make-work, don't you?" she said to me, as if she really wasn't sure if I knew that or not.

"Obviously," I said. "Our real work doesn't start until we reach the homestead. In the meantime, it's important to not lose the practice of working every day."

"Sure, but shouldn't you be doing something *useful*?" she pressed.

I paused in my sorting, intrigued. "Like what?" Then a sudden thought struck me. "You think we should just have afternoon prayers as well as morning prayers?" That would be the very definition of useful.

"Ugh. *No*," Ms. Ardala said. And I remembered being vaguely aware during morning prayers how Ms. Ardala and Mr. Spectre had at first watched us in quiet amusement before… just sort of wandering off. I wasn't sure how that was possible, given that we were all in the same room.

In my defense, my eyes had been closed.

"Well, what, then?" I asked. "Kolya is monitoring things from the command room, but even if there are tasks to be done in there, he's told us we're not allowed in there, so we can't help with that. And he brings out our ration for dinnertime, so there's nothing to cook. Maybe they'll be some cleaning at some point, but since we aren't cooking or preparing food, that really won't be much. Trust me."

"I do trust you," Ms. Ardala said. "Absolutely you know more about all of that than I. No argument there."

"Did you want a task?" I asked. I knew I should be offering to share my work with her, but I really didn't want to. If we got done twice as fast, we'd just have to dump it all back into the tray and start again. And then it would feel like fake work to me too, not just Ms. Ardala.

Which was weird. Wasn't it fake in the first place?

I pushed that thought aside and looked to Ms. Ardala, who hadn't yet answered me.

"I think Mr. Spectre and I will find our own ways to be useful," she said.

"That sounds lovely," I said with a smile.

But I didn't really understand what she meant until the next morning, when we all awoke to find the two of them standing over us in our bedrolls, grinning with a manic kind of glee.

"That," Mr. Spectre said at once, pointing to the odd door-shaped thing I hadn't even looked at since first waking up, "is a fake airlock."

"What do you mean?" Brother August asked as he rubbed at his eyes.

"The panel that is meant to be the controls?" Ms. Ardala said then went over to it to sweep her arm in front of it in a displaying sort of motion, like she was about to try to sell it to us for some exorbitant amount.

"Isn't functional," Mr. Spectre finished for her.

"Well, this does appear to be an older model of ship," Brother

August said. "Perhaps it's merely broken. It's not like it matters. We have no use for it, even on the long road."

"It's not broken," Mr. Spectre said, then pulled it off the wall with ridiculous ease. Shouldn't it have been bolted into the bulkhead more firmly than that? Then he showed us the back side. A few connectors dangled, neatly tied the way equipment came when new from the factory. The ties had never been cut. Nothing had ever been connected.

I looked around the room again, really looked. I had never left the commune, sure, but I had read a few books. Seen a few vids. I wasn't entirely clueless.

But I still wasn't sure why everything felt wrong.

"Again, it isn't necessary for what we're doing," Brother August said. "Kolya has been transporting people across the stars for quite some time. I would assume he never finished installing the things he knew he wouldn't need."

"Why assume when you can ask him, though?" Mr. Spectre pressed.

"Because it's going to be a long journey made even longer if we wear his patience any thinner than it already is," Brother August said.

"Ha. Well done," Mr. Spectre said, and tossed the control panel into a corner.

"It sounds reasonable enough, that plan. Doesn't it, Mr. Spectre?" Ms. Ardala said.

"Sounds reasonable enough," Mr. Spectre allowed.

"Only you should probably tell him that other bit," Ms. Ardala said, wincing ever so slightly as if she really didn't want him to.

"I suppose I should, Ms. Ardala," he agreed.

"What's the other bit?" Brother August asked when the pause stretched on too long.

Then I suddenly knew what was about to be said. Something just clicked, and I blurted out, "we're not in a spaceship."

My five commune companions all turned to gape at me. But Mr. Spectre was grinning that manic grin at me, touching his nose with the finger of one hand and pointing at me with the other. Ms. Ardala just looked quietly impressed.

"What ever do you mean, Sister June?" Sister April asked me.

"Just, doesn't this feel all wrong for a spaceship?" I said.

"Well, only Brother August has ever been on a spaceship before," Sister April said.

"And I was in cold sleep the entire time, there and back again," Brother August said. "I never even saw the ships that transported me."

"That's probably deliberate," Mr. Spectre said with a shrug. "Because this isn't a spaceship at all. I would say what we're actually standing in is nothing more than a shipping container. The kind that transport entire colonies across the Solar System. They had a whole lot of them stacked in an arm of the spaceport back on Earth."

"A shipping container?" Brother August said skeptically.

"Hence the fake airlock," Mr. Spectre said. "If it looked like the regular door it is, you wouldn't be afraid to go out of it without a suit. And I'm guessing none of you have suits."

"But this is ridiculous," Brother August said. "Are you contending we've never left the spaceport on Earth?"

"Not a bit!" Mr. Spectre said. "Just that, whatever else Kolya is doing, he's not flying us anywhere himself."

"No, of course not," Brother August said. "He was meant to be in cold sleep with the rest of us."

"So who is flying?" Mr. Spectre asked.

"Only Kolya knows for sure," Ms. Ardala said with a grin.

Brother August licked his lips nervously, then looked to the rest of us. "Come, brothers and sisters. It's time for us to pray. And I think we all know what we should focus our prayers on now."

Mr. Spectre groaned and threw up his hands dramatically, but neither he nor Ms. Ardala attempted to stop the rest of us from praying.

But as we were praying, I was sure I could hear them digging through our supplies, searching for something. They were quiet about it, but only so as not to disturb us. They weren't being secretive.

Not even when they went out that door they said was a fake airlock. I heard the clang of it opening just as Brother August's droning chant was leading us out of our prayerful minds back to ordinary wakefulness. I opened my eyes and saw the two of them wearing environmental suits. With the helmets on, I could no longer tell them apart.

But one of them waved to me before closing the door behind them with an even louder clang.

All I had seen behind them was a second door like the first. But airlocks would have heavier doors, with sealing mechanisms or something, wouldn't they?

I ran to the door and wrestled it open, half expecting to feel the pull of air rushing out the far side, sucking the two of them in their inadequate suits out into the black. But all I saw was the second door, closed once more. The two of them were gone.

The afternoon was endless, my assigned task of checking the seams of all the packed garments for places in need of repair even more pointless than sorting the hardware had been. I hadn't even made any work first. I was just… doing something pointless.

I was just beginning to think about that swallow of gel that was awaiting me at the end of this endless day when the door banged open again, making us all jump. Mr. Spectre and Ms. Ardala bustled inside, closing the door behind them before pulling off their helmets. They were both bright-eyed and pink-cheeked with excitement.

"You'll never believe where we are!" Mr. Spectre said at once.

"They'll never believe it, Mr. Spectre," Ms. Ardala said. "They'll have to see it to believe it."

"Do you really think so?" Mr. Spectre said. For once, he sounded like he was really asking Ms. Ardala a question, not just setting up the next round in their banter. But before she could answer, Kolya emerged from the other door with his tray of cups.

Then he saw the two of them standing there and scowled. His eyes swept over the pressure suits they were wearing and his scowl deepened. Then he noticed where they were standing, but the door that no longer sported a fake control panel, and the scowl became something frighteningly intense.

"What is going on here?" he demanded in a low whisper that shook me more than a shout would have.

"We know where we are, Mr. Kolya," Mr. Spectre said.

"We've seen it," Ms. Ardala said.

"Where are we?" Brother August asked. But he was asking Kolya.

"Well, you know precisely where we are. We are en route to that shiny new home of yours," he blustered, his face red.

"That's generally where we are, sure," Mr. Spectre said. "Not *precisely*."

"No, where we are precisely is on somebody else's ship," Ms. Ardala said.

"Or some*thing*'s ship," Mr. Spectre corrected her. She accepted this amendment with a tilt of her head and a nod.

"Well, how else do you think we do it?" Kolya demanded. "No human ship can travel these distances."

"Whose ship are we on, Mr. Kolya?" Brother August asked calmly.

But Kolya ignored him. He was too busy glaring at the smirking Mr. Spectre. "You can't go back out there. It's forbidden. Absolutely forbidden."

"Like going into your room is forbidden?" Ms. Ardala asked with innocence even I could tell was feigned.

"Exactly!" Kolya said. But then his eyes narrowed in suspicion. "Wait, have you been in the command room?"

"Have we?" Ms. Ardala asked Mr. Spectre, still sweetly innocent.

"You know, I think we have," Mr. Spectre said.

"That was forbidden! Absolutely forbidden!" Kolya said.

"So you mentioned," Mr. Spectre said.

"You swore to follow the rules!" Kolya said.

Mr. Spectre laughed out loud. "I think you'll find it was someone else who promised you that."

"Indeed, it was before we ever found the stowaways, Mr. Kolya," Brother August said. "I think you'll agree, when I made that promise to you, I was only speaking on behalf of the six of us from the Church commune."

"But this is ridiculous!" Kolya sputtered. Then some other thought struck him and his eyes narrowed further still. He stepped up close to Mr. Spectre, towering over him as they stood toe-to-toe. Mr. Spectre looked completely unbothered. "What did you do?" Kolya hissed at him.

Mr. Spectre blinked. "Do?"

"When you were in my command room, what did you do? What

did you touch?" Kolya said, his voice still low. Although how he hoped to keep any secrets now, I had no clue.

"We didn't touch any of your dummy controls," Ms. Ardala assured him. I thought she was making a disparaging remark, but then I remembered the airlock panel that had never been connected. So he had a whole control room that was just for show?

"What *did* you touch?" Kolya demanded, spinning to tower over her. But she, too, was unbothered. She just blinked up at him innocently through the locks of her magenta hair.

"Well, we might have touched the food a bit," Mr. Spectre said suddenly, as if just remembering.

"You took rations?" Brother August demanded.

"As lovely as that gel stuff is, no," Ms. Ardala said. "But Kolya hasn't been taking it either, have you, Kolya?"

"What are they talking about, Kolya?" Brother August asked.

Kolya glowered down at Ms. Ardala but said nothing.

"The company Kolya works for amply stocked this transport for the entire journey, even the sizable chunk of it we all spent in cold sleep before the juice was depleted," Mr. Spectre said. Then he gave Brother August a sincerely sorrowful look. "Sorry about that. Math was never my strong suit."

"You've already been forgiven for that, my son," Brother August said, almost formally. But then gave himself a little shake and fixed a hard stare at Kolya again. "But tell me what it is that we don't know."

"Allow me," Ms. Ardala said as she reached for the opening mechanism for the door that wasn't an airlock. "This thing we're in looks like a shipping container because it is a shipping container," she said as she slowly eased the door open.

"But I rather doubt the aliens giving us a lift even know we're here," Mr. Spectre went on, then stopped to bark out a laugh. "Irony, right? Kolya has such strong feelings about stowaways, and yet that's what we all are."

"Hiding in the walls of an alien ship," Ms. Ardala said, easing the door just a little bit further open, but still not far enough for me or anyone else to see what was beyond it.

"In the walls?" Brother August repeated, pressing a trembling hand to his forehead. "Just how large are these aliens?"

"Huge," Ms. Ardala said gleefully. "So big I almost think they wouldn't even notice us if we ran out into their halls."

"Not that we would do such a thing," Mr. Spectre said.

"Well, we might," Ms. Ardala corrected him. "If there was something we very much wanted to have."

"Oh, you mean like all the *real* food someone's been hoarding?" Mr. Spectre said.

Then Ms. Ardala threw the door open wide. The far door was open as well, and what lay beyond was mostly darkness, but there were patches of light. It did indeed look like an immense corridor in a ship, lit for the night shift with only enough light to avoid tripping in the dark.

I mean, the corridor itself was larger than the dome that housed our commune back on Mars. Quite a bit larger. I had never seen a space so large, and I had visited the canyons of Mars once as a child.

Then I noticed something else. Food. Piles and piles of it, sitting in one of those patches of light in the distance.

"We unpacked your crates for you," Mr. Spectre said to Kolya. "Maybe you didn't notice? We slid it all out the 'airlock' in the command room before heading out ourselves."

"I don't think he noticed," Ms. Ardala said, her eyes dancing with delight.

"I was going to share," Kolya said, but not a one of us actually believed him. He must have guessed that because he quickly amended his statement. "I'm *going* to share. We just need to bring that all back in and we'll share and share alike. Right?"

"What about the aliens?" Brother August asked.

"Oh, I'm sure they won't notice if we're quick," Kolya said with a laugh that was far from convincing. "I mean, it looks like their night shift and all. And these two have been out there all day, apparently."

"Not quite all day," Ms. Ardala said.

"But you all sure do shut out the world when you pray," Mr. Spectre said.

"Thank you," Sister April said, although I don't think he had precisely meant it as a compliment.

"Look at all that food," Kolya said. "It's too much for just me."

Brother August said nothing, just raised a single eyebrow, and let Kolya figure out just how bad what he had just said sounded.

"I mean, more than I can carry back. Someone has to help me," he said.

"Why don't you show us how safe it all is, and then we'll see about volunteers," Mr. Spectre said.

"I don't trust you," Kolya said lowly.

"That's probably the wisest thing I've ever heard you say," Mr. Spectre said. For once, there was no jaunty humor in his voice or in his eyes. I felt a chill run up my spine and was very grateful his ire wasn't being directed at me.

"Fine," Kolya said, swinging his arms as if warming up for a sport. "Fine. I'll go. Fine."

"I'll hold the door for you, love," Ms. Ardala said.

He glared at her, but said nothing. For the longest moment, nothing happened.

Then all at once, he was sprinting. I would never have guessed a man of Kolya's size could run like that. I doubted he could do it far, and indeed he seemed winded when he reached the pile of food.

He looked it over in a way that was instantly familiar to me. I had seen him do the same, when I had just woken from cold sleep. That was when he had taken all of our food. *Our* food, not his.

Then he picked up one of the boxes. He started to turn to run back to us, but something was wrong. He stopped, shaking the box in his hands with a puzzled look.

Mr. Spectre and Ms. Ardala exchanged a smile but said nothing.

Kolya turned back to the pile, sorting through the boxes. I realized from the way they were flying about that they were all empty. The stowaways had opened the packing crates, removed the boxes with brightly colored labels, then put the contents of the boxes back into the crates.

All just to create an irresistible trap.

Kolya started to rage, but he was too far away for any of us to hear him. Then he threw up his arms in exasperation and started sprinting back towards us. Without food to lure him on, he was running much more slowly.

He was still running when something rolled down the corridor. It wasn't remotely humanoid. It looked, if anything, like a giant gelatinous wheel, covered in hairy tentacles. I only got a momentary glimpse of it, and then it was gone.

And so was Kolya. I could see a long streak where he had once been, but no more.

Ms. Ardala closed the door and spun the mechanism shut.

"Now," Mr. Spectre said, clapping his hands and then rubbing them together with relish. "Who's hungry for some real food?"

THE FAIR FOLK

Every midsummer, for as far back as Peter Fisher could recall, his family had gotten up before dawn to make the long walk to the top of the highest hill that overlooked the nearest village to his family's farm and visit the fair. His siblings always looked forward to this day with breathless anticipation. His sisters— well, all of his sisters save Elinor—would chat together as they worked in the kitchen about what they would buy with the coins they had saved all year. His brothers would dare each other to attempt the feats the acrobatic performers had done the year before, and wonder how they would top their old tricks this year.

Peter had never cared much for the fair. He didn't like the noise of crowds, or the heat from all the bodies pressed close all around him. He didn't like the smells of so many different kinds of food being cooked all at once, and so close to where the animals stood in pens, waiting to be bought or sold. Elinor had once used her saved pennies to buy some kind of chewy candy that smelled like roses. She had let him try a little, and that had been all right, but Peter would've preferred eating it back at the farm, just him and his sister sitting on the hillside with the clean smell of sun-baked grass all around them, and the buzzing of bees, and maybe the rustling of a breeze through the grass.

But this year, Peter was the first one up in the dark hours before dawn, dressed and ready before the others had even stumbled out of bed. He was so anxious, he even waited outside the door for the rest of the family to finish the porridge his mother had left in its pot nestled among the embers of the fire the night before. He wasn't hungry. He just wanted to go. He could barely stand to wait.

When his siblings finally emerged from the house, his parents close behind, he longed to start running along the trail that would lead them to the fair. But he didn't. Instead, he watched his brothers and most of his sisters rush past him, chatting about what they wanted to see and what they hoped to buy. Then he watched as his parents passed him, almost as if they didn't notice him standing there. But they were distracted, his mother checking her basket and his father checking his satchel to make sure nothing they had hoped to sell had been left behind.

Which left only Elinor, lingering uncertainly just outside the door. She blinked at the night sky, but whatever might be passing through her mind didn't show at all on her face.

These days, it never did.

Not since the fair the year before.

"Come on, Elinor. Take my hand," Peter said. But he had to take hers instead, then pull her along after him. Her hand in his was so cold, and far bonier than he remembered.

He had been forgetting too much to tell her to eat. She wouldn't do it if he didn't keep asking her to.

But it would be okay. Peter was going to fix everything. He would get his sister back.

They plodded along after the rest of the family as the world brightened around them. The eastern sky faded from dark blue to light as the stars winked out. Then that blue became a rosy pink, and Peter pulled up the hood of his jerkin. Not that he was cold. He just needed to pull the faded leather down low over his eyes. The sun was too bright. He knew it was going to hurt his eyes the instant it emerged over the hills ahead, but he had to be outside today. He had to.

Still, he flinched when the first rays stabbed in under the hem of his hood, all the way to the back of his skull, or so it felt like. Elinor stopped walking, but didn't ask if he was okay. She only stood there, holding his hand, and gazing at him with those vacant eyes.

"It's all right, Eli," he said, squeezing her hand. "Let's go. We'll be there by midmorning if we don't slow down. The sooner the better, Eli."

She just looked back at him, but when he started walking again, she fell into step beside him, not making him pull her along.

He had been waiting all year for this moment. Ever since the night of the fair the year before. After he'd finally found Elinor again. She'd disappeared almost as soon as they'd arrived, and it was well past sunset before they found her again.

And his parents are never once seemed even a little worried.

"She's a sensible girl, Peter," his father had told him. "She knows how to keep herself out of trouble, and she knows how to find our farm."

Which had terrified him, the idea that they would leave the fair without her. But in the end, they hadn't had to. One minute they were saying goodbye to the other families they knew also mingling at the fair, prying his other sisters away from their friends, getting his brothers to stop wrestling with each other, and Peter's heart had been racing fast, not sure how he was going to confront that last moment. He'd have to say something. He'd have to insist.

But then he'd turned and saw Elinor standing there beside him, just as suddenly as she had disappeared that morning. He'd been so happy to see her again, he'd thrown his arms around her and hugged her tight.

Peter would let Elinor and sometimes their mother hug him, but he'd never in his life been the one to start a hug. He was prepared to be embarrassed when Elinor teased him about it.

But Elinor didn't say anything at all. And the bare skin of her arms was so cold.

"She's just tired," his mother had assured him.

And the next day, when she was still strangely quiet with that vacant look in her eyes, his mother had told him, "your sister will be a woman soon. That can be a strange time for a girl. Don't be so hard on her."

That answer didn't satisfy Peter at all. Elinor was barely a year older than he was, and he didn't feel remotely like he would be a man soon. Besides, Elinor was no more like their older sisters than he was like their older brothers. Not that they were like each other, either. But Peter had never minded being quiet and easy to miss when Elinor had been there to talk for him. And he didn't mind that everyone thought he was moody, because Elinor had known he wasn't, really.

Anyway, Peter didn't think he'd been hard on her. He hadn't asked her to tell him any of her stories at bedtime, even though she'd never missed a night before, never even once. And he hadn't asked her to sing any of the songs she made up while they worked together weeding the gardens. Not even when weeding became harvesting, and harvesting became preserving, and the skies turned gray and the snows came.

Not even then.

But he knew she wasn't right. She never smiled, and she was always cold. His parents didn't notice. Maybe having so many children and being so busy all the time made noticing the change in one child all but impossible. Especially when that change just made her quieter, while his other siblings were as loud as ever.

But Peter noticed. And he noticed when she stopped brushing her hair, or washing her face, or eating her food. So he did all those things for her.

And no one noticed that either.

But late one night as Peter slept in his little bed in the little curtained-off corner of the loft that the two of them shared, he heard her mumbling in her sleep. He couldn't understand her. It sounded like words, but no words he knew.

Still, he climbed out of his bed and sat on hers and held her cold, bony hand, and asked her over and over to tell him what she had seen at the fair. She had been on her own without their family for an entire day. What had she seen?

It was a warm night in early spring when she finally mumbled out an answer to his question, an answer he could understand.

A blue tent. A blue tent with gold trim. She had looked and looked for years and years and finally found it.

Then she sank into a deeper sleep, and no matter how many times Peter whispered to her in the night, she never talked in her sleep again.

But that was all right, Peter reminded himself, squeezing her numb hand in his as they reached the last of the hills between their farm and the fair. That was all right, because he knew what to look for now. A blue tent with gold trim.

Then the path took one last turn and he could see the flags and tents of the fair there on top of the highest hill, shining too bright in the midmorning sun. It hurt to look at. So many colors, so many patterns in the walls of the tents. Everyone wearing their most colorful clothing.

And the sounds, and the smells, and the unevenness of the churned-up earth underfoot.

Peter closed his eyes and bit down hard on his lip, hard enough to taste his own blood on his tongue.

He had to get through this.

He gave himself a nod, then opened his eyes.

He could do this. He could find that tent, even though it meant pushing his way through the throngs of people with all their smells and sounds and just the sticky feel of them.

But he didn't think he should take Elinor with him. He wasn't sure what he'd find there, and he might not be able to do whatever needed doing there and take care of her at the same time.

He moved her closer to their mother, then grabbed a fistful of the back of her skirt. He closed Elinor's hand around it, then let her go. He was afraid her hand would drop away, but it didn't. She held on tight. And his mother—deep in conversation with a woman at the first stall they'd come to, arguing about the price of buttons—didn't notice her daughter clinging to her.

And she didn't notice when Peter slipped away.

Pushing through the crowds was exactly as awful as he'd known it'd be. And the day was hot, even for midsummer. Everyone was sweating, and the air was too still to blow away any of the smells. And it only got hotter as the sun passed its zenith and started its long, lazy descent towards the west.

And still, Peter hadn't seen anything remotely like a blue tent with gold trim.

When he couldn't stand it anymore, he broke away from the crowd. He skipped gingerly over tent pegs and ropes, finding a respite in the narrow gap between two tents. He knew he wasn't the first person to find this place. Someone had left the contents of their stomach here, bits of meat still clinging to the ropes, the sour smell of regurgitated beer eye-wateringly strong.

But it was quieter there, so Peter went further in, away from the smell. Now the voices from the crowds were a mere murmur in the background. Then that too was gone as Peter clambered over more ropes and tent pegs, past tent after tent.

Then finally he was back out on a patch of bare earth that had been churned up by the feet of people and the hooves of sheep and goats and pigs being driven to and from the pens. But there was no sign of a single other living soul now. There was no smell of food grilling in the open air. And it was so quiet, Peter almost felt like he could hear a humming coming from the sun that was beating down on his shoulders.

But the heat didn't distract him now. Because he'd found it. A tent of blue, a deep shade of indigo with highlights and lowlights within it that seemed to swirl together even as he looked at it. Like he was staring into a stream-fed pool, although no water he had ever seen had been close to this shade of blue. Not even the sky had ever been so blue.

And the gold trim that ran along every seam in the tent walls was not just gold-colored tassels. It was real gold, shining in the sunlight too brightly for Peter to look directly at it. Real gold, but cast into wires so fine it could be worked like thread, spun together into trim and tassels.

It was exactly what he had pictured when Elinor had whispered to him in the night. Exactly. Only she hadn't described it at all, really. All she had said was a blue tent with gold trim. And yet he had known exactly how it had stood taller than all the other tents, how the indigo color of the walls had swirled like whirlpools, how the gold had shone in the sunlight.

He had been here before.

But when? To his regret, he had never gone to look for Elinor when she had disappeared the year before. When else could he have seen this place?

A breeze blew down the lane, too hot to be welcome, but at least it wasn't carrying any of the fair smells with it. But it set the tent flaps rustling. The other tents in the fair all had their flaps tied back, leaving the interiors open and inviting to all the passersby. This one was closed, and yet that little rustle in the breeze seemed to be drawing Peter closer.

He crossed the lane and grasped the edge of one of the flaps. He pulled it aside, just a little, but not enough. He couldn't see anything inside.

"Young master Peter Fisher. Do come in." The voice came from within the tent. It sounded quite close, close enough where he should be able to see the speaker, but he could not. He couldn't even tell if the voice came from a man or a woman. One moment he thought the one, but then he thought the other. But, unidentified as it was, it still felt so familiar. Like it was a voice that had sung lullabies to him as a babe. Night after night, all night long.

He touched his tongue to where he had bitten into his lip before. It felt fat and hot and still tasted faintly of blood, like rusty metal. It made him feel stronger, somehow, that metallic taste.

He pushed his way inside the tent.

It was cooler on the inside, dark and cool like his mother's root cellar. He stood just inside the doorway, just out of reach of the hot sun, and breathed in air that was gently perfumed by the petals of some flower he couldn't name. His sweaty skin broke out in goose-flesh, and the places where his shirt clung wetly to him were suddenly so cold he shivered.

"Poor Master Peter. You've never adjusted to the world above, have you?" a different voice said. Again, I couldn't guess whether the speaker was a man or a woman, but this time when I looked around, I could see them in the shadows at the back of the tent. Their face was so pale it glowed, and their eyes sparkled like they were cast from silver.

Peter touched his tongue to the split in his lip again, then said, "I'm here about my sister."

"We know why you are here, young Master Peter," the first voice said. Then Peter saw a second form emerging from the shadows, as pale and silvery as the first. He realized the long garments they wore were the same swimming indigo as the tent walls around them.

The tent walls that let not a bit of sunlight peek through the weave.

"Our lady awaits you, young Master Peter," the second voice said. They made a sweeping gesture, and Peter realized that the tent was not one tent but two, joined at a doorway. The first person to speak mirrored the sweeping gesture.

Peter looked from one pale face to the other, but it was like every time he had looked at Elinor over the last year. There was no expression to be read there, not in the angle of the mouth or eyebrows, and definitely not in those inhumane eyes themselves.

He touched his tongue to his lip, but the blood taste was gone. He bit down on it again, just enough to split again where it had scabbed over. Only a drop or two of blood emerged, but it was enough. His head felt a little clearer. And somehow, his head feeling clearer made the perfumed-scented air shift from lovely to cloying.

But at least it wasn't hot.

"Our lady awaits," the first speaker said, with just a hint of an edge of warning to their voice.

Peter nodded, balled his hands into fists, and took the few steps between the gesturing arms, through the double folds of the tent doorways, and into the tent beyond, all in a rush.

It had looked like it would be even darker in the inner chamber, but when he emerged into it, he found it bathed in a soft golden light. A single glowing orb hung from the highest point of the tent above. It was like the winter sun, dim and far away, but still welcome.

"Young Master Peter Fisher," the woman, for this time it was clearly a woman speaking, said to him. She was sitting on a golden chair with her equally golden hair spilling over the back and arms of the chair to pool on the carpeted floor all around her. Her eyes were green, but not like any eyes he'd ever seen in a person. They were too gleaming, too emerald-like.

Too unkind.

"You've come to ask me a boon," she prompted him. Her face was warmer than her servants, with even a hint of pink to her cheeks. But like them, she showed no expression.

Although he thought she was thinking and feeling something all the same. Not like his sister. His sister's face was blank because her mind was blank. But this woman's mind was not blank at all. She just didn't choose to let him see inside.

"I want you to fix what you did to my sister," he said, then flicked his tongue over the wound in his lip again.

He thought maybe the woman flinched when he did that. Or maybe she didn't. Her face never changed, and her hands remained resting lightly on the arms of her chair, just as they'd been before.

Still, he thought he'd seen something. Maybe.

Or maybe not.

"Your sister," the lady said consideringly.

"Elinor Fisher," he said. "She came here a year ago, and you found her. I know you did."

"Don't you mean *she* found *me*?" she asked.

"No," Peter said. He knew what he'd meant.

"I don't give a boon without receiving something in return," she told him.

"Anything," Peter said.

Too quickly. Like the flinch, he wasn't entirely certain he had seen her smirk. Her face hadn't changed, and he had been gazing at her without blinking. Still, he thought she had.

"What I give to her I must take from you," she said. "That is the price."

She didn't exactly sound regretful, although she did sound like she was implying someone not her had set that price.

"I know," Peter said. "Just do it. Please," he quickly added, when those emerald eyes finally showed an actual emotion, narrowing at him with such cold contempt he was shivering all over again.

"Come closer," she said, lifting her hands from the armrests to gesture him closer. He took a step, but she kept gesturing, so he took another. The third step brought him toe-to-toe with her. He had to look up at her, even standing as he was and sitting as she was.

It was like she was pulling all the warmth from his body. He was shaking so hard his teeth were chattering together. He squeezed his fists again, but couldn't make the shivering stop.

He couldn't part his teeth to let his tongue touch his lip again.

He stopped shivering the instant her hands closed over his upper arms, but only because he was suddenly frozen in place. His tongue pressed against the backs of his teeth, but he couldn't command them to open.

She leaned down closer, that warmth-sucking feeling growing as she did so to something acutely painful. Then her lips touched his forehead like the searing touch of cold metal on a winter's day.

And then she was gone. Not just not touching him; she was no longer inside the tent. Peter stood alone before an empty golden chair under a dim golden light.

That light grew dimmer still, or the shadows grew darker, or perhaps both at once. He felt a momentary panic. It was too much like the light was leaving because he was underwater, being pulled deeper and deeper, farther and farther from light and warmth and air.

He opened his mouth to cry out, but realized before he made a sound that he could touch that bloody spot on his lip again.

He did so. And he felt better. The world around him was no brighter, but that was all right. He was inside a tent. It was supposed to be dark.

He went out into the outer chamber to find the servants too had disappeared without a trace. Then he was out in the lane, standing on the churned-up earth. He started to panic again, finding everything still dark.

But it was only because the sun had set. He had been inside the tent far longer than he had thought.

He found the gap in the tents he had come through before and worked his way back towards the sounds of the fair, back towards the smell of beer vomit. He supposed it should be welcoming, those sounds and smells as he rejoined the crowds of people still milling around the fair by torchlight. He was back where he belonged.

But it wasn't welcoming. It was, however, a bit more tolerable.

Peter looked around to get his bearings. He was most likely to find his parents at the open field on the north end of the fair, where the meat was still cooking in the many open pits, filling the air with smoke and the charred smell of blackened flesh.

He had just decided on a direction to go when arms closed around him from the other way, pulling him into a tight embrace.

A warm embrace.

"Peter!" Elinor cried as she squeezed him tighter still. He fought the urge to struggle free. As much as he'd longed for her to want to hug him again, now that he'd gotten what he wanted, it was rather a lot to suffer through.

But he did. He even patted her on the shoulder a little, if awkwardly. She was pinning his arms to his sides. It was hard to reach.

Then, in the blink of an eye, she went from crushing him close to thrusting him an arm's-length away. She even shook him a little.

"You never should've done that!" she said crossly.

"I had to!" he said. "Nothing was right when you were wrong."

She had been about to blast more words at him, he could tell. But then she just closed her mouth again, looking at him half in fury and half in… something else. Sorrow, maybe?

"Petey, I'm so sorry," she said. Then she blinked back tears, and he realized he had been right. She was still sad.

"She said it was all fixed now," he said. "You're supposed to be better."

"I *am* better, Petey," Elinor said, then gave him another quick hug to prove her point. She was warm and talking to him. She'd probably even sing, if he asked her to.

"Then why are you still sad?" he asked.

"It took me years to find that place," she said. "Years and years. And they didn't want to let me exchange my happiness for yours. Not even though it was a perfectly good bargain. They made me *earn* the right to bargain with them first. I… I'm not going to talk about that, Peter. Ever."

"Okay," Peter said, but he was confused.

"You ruined my bargain, Peter!" she said, with such big-sister frustration that he knew what he had really done. He had fixed her. She was herself again.

"You shouldn't have made a bargain with them in the first place," Peter said. "Don't you know what they are?"

"No, not really. And you don't either!" she told him.

Peter shrugged. That was true. He didn't really know what they were. But that wasn't the point. No, the point had more to do with what she'd just said, about exchanging happinesses. "Why would you trade away your happiness? I didn't need it. It was a stupid trade."

"It was not!" she said. But then she stopped being angry long enough to peer at him closely. "You really didn't feel any different? I mean, when I gave up my happiness, it was like all the color washed out of the world. Music didn't sound like anything at all. Nothing tasted sweet or rich or anything. I couldn't even smell flowers or, you know, that smell when Mom hugs us. It all just went away."

Then she was angry again, shoving Peter hard enough in both shoulders that he had to stagger back several steps to avoid falling over.

"And then it all came back! All the colors were there, and the smells and the tastes even. Right there in the middle of the fair!" She had thrown up her hands in emphasis, but now she was pointing an accusing finger at him. "And I knew what you had done."

"So, it worked, then," Peter said. He didn't understand why she was so angry.

"You shouldn't have done it," she said, but quietly now. Like she was tired. He was tired too, he supposed. "You just shouldn't have."

"I don't understand why you were looking for them in the first place," Peter said.

She looked at him sharply, like she thought he was joking with her, and she didn't find it remotely funny. Then she looked at him more closely, uncomfortably closely.

Peter took a step back.

"You don't remember at all?" she whispered.

He just shrugged, not sure what she was even talking about.

"Peter, they found you first," she said, still low, as if afraid someone would overhear them. Someone in the roaring crowd of people who had been drinking tankards of beer all day long and now into the night.

But he was whispering too when he said, "no, it was you. Last year."

"No, Peter, it was you," she insisted. "You were just a kid, barely big enough to walk at the time, so I guess you don't remember. But I do. I was supposed to be watching you. Not all day, of course. I was just a little kid myself. But all the older kids were gone off somewhere, and it was just me and you and Mom, and she needed to bargain with someone in one of the stalls. So she put your hand in mine and said, 'don't let go of his hand, Eli.' And I didn't mean to, but I guess I did."

Peter didn't say anything. He didn't remember this at all.

But he had remembered the tent. And the lady.

"We found you that night, but you were never the same," she said, sad again. He was afraid she was going to start crying again.

"I don't remember ever being different," Peter said. "To me, this is how I am. This is my 'the same'."

"Truly?" she asked, blinking back tears. "You didn't feel all the colors wash away when she… did what she did?"

Peter thought about it very carefully, then shook his head. "No. It was more like, everything went back to normal. Everything before was wrong. But this is as it should be."

"You don't miss being happy?" she pressed.

He thought again, then shook his head again. "I wasn't happy when you weren't, Elinor. I promise I wasn't. Please don't try to find them again. They can't fix anything, really. I just am who I am now. But this is what it feels like to be me. I'm me."

He didn't think he was making any sense, but she smiled at him all the same and gave him one last hug.

He let her do it.

Then she took his hand and guided him through the crowds to where the rest of their family waited.

THE ROD OF CIRCE

Everything seemed in order, ready to go for the weekly support group meeting of the Victims of That Bastard Magician Samson. The chairs were arranged in a circle that Kitty Chilton hoped conveyed coziness despite the cold dampness of the cellar, particularly during a spring as rainy as the one they were having this year.

She would prefer to meet upstairs in her bookshop, in the open area among the shelves that she set aside for readings and discussion groups. The smell was better up there, the dry musty smell of antique books infinitely preferable to the wet musty smell down here that seemed to warn of malicious mold spreading in the cracks in the stone walls or just out of sight in the shadows of the slanted boards that held up the low ceiling. The places the dim bulbs never reached.

But Kitty had been outvoted. Her bookshop, which barely did enough business to keep her alive, was still too public a place.

That Bastard Magician Samson might find them. Or so just over half of the members thought. And so, the cellar it was.

But whether or not the circle of chairs conveyed coziness, Kitty fretted that there just weren't enough of them. Every week brought more people seeking support for the sudden unwelcome changes to their lives. Even after four other groups had started meeting in other parts of the Hidden City that lurked in the magic-laden corners of Minneapolis, unseen to the mundane world, there were still new people finding their way to her cellar nearly every meeting.

Well, if they needed more chairs, she had them. She couldn't move them herself, being noncorporeal, little more than a living ghost, thanks to That Bastard Magician Samson. But she could direct the others to where they were tucked in the storage space under the rickety old staircase. Another shadowy place the light never reached, but there all the same.

But she was really more worried that she hadn't ordered enough snacks. Again.

Kitty hovered over the refreshment table, not quite literally. Despite the curse that Bastard Magician Samson had cast on her three years before, the one that kept her from touching people and things, she still maintained a working relationship with floors.

Then she heard other feet on those stairs, and knew from the quick, skipping gait that it was Lara Tilley even before she turned to see the young woman ducking under the support beam that hung head-crackingly low just at the bottom of the steps.

"Hi! Good to see you!" Kitty said, but Lara just nodded.

Of course, that was all she *could* do. That Bastard Magician Samson had taken her voice more than two years back.

Lara crossed the room to her favorite chair, the one next to Kitty's where both of them would be the first to see anyone who came down the stairs. She set a tall paper cup on her chair, the coffee chain's famous logo just discernable over the top of the cardboard sleeve that kept the contents from scalding her palm while she carried it. Then she went to the refreshment table to use the coffeemaker's hot water feature to make herself a cup of tea using a tea bag she pulled out of her own pocket.

"I wonder how many new people will come? What with the rain and all," Kitty said as she settled more or less into her chair. Chairs weren't like floors; they didn't feel solid to her. But if she stayed focused, she could hold a squat position that would look like sitting to the others.

Lara blew out a sighing breath, tipped her head to one side with an inquisitive look on her face, then shrugged.

Lara hadn't learned any sign language since being cursed. Kitty suspected that would feel too much like giving in to her new situation, and Lara was one of the ones who truly believed that someone, someday would reverse everything That Bastard Magician Samson had done. Kitty, herself, had no such hopes.

Instead of signing, Lara *could* make her phone speak for her, typing in words and using text-to-speech to "speak" to others. She had gone through an array of different voices, trying out American woman or Australian man or whatever.

But in the end, her expressive pantomimes were her usual form of conversation. That, and her endless array of T-shirts. Today's example was a black baby doll T with "Self-Rescuing Princess" written on it in bright spangly letters. The P was even wearing a little crown.

Kitty understood the impulse. She just didn't always understand Lara.

"Wow, the fourth straight day of deluge. Are we sure he didn't curse the weather this time?" Jodi Fletcher grumped as she stomped down the stairs, shaking water droplets off of her raincoat before hanging it on one of the hooks on the wall. She touched her frosted blonde hair gingerly, but the rain hadn't stood a chance against the shellacking of hair product that held those curls arranged just so.

Lara went to her chair, exchanging the tea for the coffee waiting on the seat. The barista's scrawls on the side of the coffee were largely indecipherable to Kitty, but they were voluminous. Lara held the coffee out to Jodi as she joined the circle. Jodi's grumpiness faded at once, and she took the mug with a murmur of thanks. Then she took a sip, grimaced, and set it aside with a sigh.

"I really appreciate it, Lara, but I just don't think we're ever going to hit on it," she said.

Lara gave her a mock-stern look, then pulled a leather-bound note-book out of her bag, checking off one in a long column of labeled boxes then showing Jodi the page.

"You have to admit, she's being very thorough," Kitty said. "She'll get it one day. Statistically, she has to."

"They add new things every day," Jody said, grumpy once more.

"But if they add something now, we already know it couldn't be what you want because it wasn't what you always ordered before," Kitty said, quite reasonably.

"They also subtract things every day," Jodi said. "What if they take away some essential part of my order, and I never get it back?"

Kitty exchanged a look with Lara. Lara kept her own expression carefully bland as she sipped at her tea, but Kitty had a harder time not letting her annoyance with Jodi show. Luckily, Jodi had turned her attention back to the coffee in her hands. It might not be her elusive preferred order, but it was good enough to keep sipping at, apparently.

Honestly, the newer people were harder and harder for Kitty to connect with. On the one hand, it was incredibly messed up how piddling and small That Bastard Magician Samson's curses were these days. Not the offenses—those had always been piddling and small and completely out of scope with the powerful curses he punished the offenders with—but the curses themselves. It was like he was losing any creativity.

But Kitty doubted that was a good sign. He might be afflicting people with more and more niche curses, but he was also afflicting more of people. And no one was stepping up to stop him.

The three of them turned at the rare sound of two sets of footsteps coming down the stairs together. That fear of being caught at a meeting usually had members avoiding each other as much as possible, especially close to the bookshop and its hidden cellar. No one wanted to be the one who accidentally lured That Bastard Magician Samson to their secret meeting space.

The first man down the stairs had to be another new victim, as he was no one Kitty knew. He didn't even look like he belonged to the world of the Hidden City, really. He looked like an accountant in the mundane world, dressed blandly in business casual, one of thousands and largely forgettable. Kitty wondered if that was, in fact, his curse. But she would know soon enough, when they shared their stories.

But the middle-aged Black man who came along behind the accountant was an old friend, the only person Kitty knew who had been cursed longer than she had. Mo Standish, escort through the hidden ways extraordinaire. Capable of leading anyone from any point in the Hidden City to any other. That was a skill set second only to the powerful ceremonial magicians in its rarity.

Or at least he had once been a professional escort through the hidden ways. Now he drove an Uber in the mundane world. The phrasing of his curse kept him from getting anywhere he wanted to go, and mostly while driving fares around, that was no conflict. He didn't want to go to any of those places, most of the time. But not all the time. Especially with restaurants as a destination, he would find himself craving the same sort of food, and that was it. He could never arrive there. When he did come to a meeting, he mostly lamented his troubles with keeping his driver rating up despite often getting lost a block away from his fare's destination.

Worse, it almost always kept him away from the meetings. Because he wanted to get there, he couldn't. He would circle the block, unable to find the door to the bookshop even as he walked past it time and time again.

But for the first time in a long time, he had made it inside.

"Hey, Kitty! Good to see you," he said, leaning down to give her an air kiss. She always liked that gesture. Such a nice way to completely ignore her own curse. "This is a new member to our little group."

"Wil Hoskins," the other man said, thrusting a hand out at Kitty. Rather than explain, she reached for his hand as if to return the gesture. But as with every other person she had done this to, he recoiled to the point of stumbling backwards when her hand passed ghost-like through his.

"Kitty Chilton," she said after Mo had finished chuckling. "I bumped into That Bastard Magician Samson three years ago. Hard enough to jostle him. I wasn't looking where I was going."

"She was carrying a tall stack of books to the back of her own book-shop," Mo said. "He could've stepped aside."

"So now you can't touch anyone?" Wil asked, aghast.

"Or any*thing*," Kitty said, trying to sound casual. Even throwing in a careless shrug.

But Mo, of course, couldn't let it go at that. "She can't even eat," he said, his voice almost a growl. "Look. She's not even touching that chair."

"Truly?" Wil said.

"If I focus, I can touch things," Kitty said. "But it's difficult to maintain for more than a minute or two."

"And then what happens?" Wil asked.

"If I was, say, trying to hold a book? It falls," Kitty said.

"And if you tried eating something?" he asked, like he couldn't help himself.

"It…falls," Kitty said. "Really, I don't think you want me to describe it. The longest I managed to hold onto food was two hours. I had a headache for days afterward just for trying, and what fell to the ground was *not* pleasant."

"Well, I feel foolish even coming here, asking for support. What I deal with is nothing compared to that," Wil said with a shake of his head.

"We all have our struggles, and we're here to help Kitty as much as the other way around," Jodi said. Kitty couldn't remember a single thing Jodi had ever done to help her, but she nodded and smiled warmly at Wil all the same.

"And you've been a help to me already," Mo said as he settled into one of the chairs with a paper cup of coffee in one hand and a cheese Danish in the other. "I don't know what your curse is, but it must be something that let you pull me inside when I'm usually doomed to circle the block on my own for the entire evening."

"Yes, well," Wil said, clearing his throat nervously. "It seems I failed to hold a door open for Mr. Samson. I mean, I didn't see him. If he called out, I didn't hear him. But apparently my profuse apologies were insufficient. Now I am cursed to hold doors open for everyone that passes by."

"And most people that pass by aren't looking to go in," Kitty guessed.

He nodded. "I work downtown. At a mundane corporation, actually. It was very difficult to explain to my boss why I'm always late."

"What did you tell him?" Mo asked.

"I told him I have OCD," Wil said.

Kitty had more questions, but stopped at the sound of another person coming down the stairs. Another newcomer. He was dressed like a mundane in dark jeans and an untucked flannel shirt, but his facial tattoos marked him as a practitioner of the highest order of ceremonial magic.

Everyone shifted around uncomfortably, not sure if they were meant to stand in his presence or even bow.

But he seemed to expect this reaction, or at least not be surprised by it. He just held up both of his hands, gesturing for them all to sit back down.

"None of that," he said. "Aren't we meant to be anonymous here?"

"That's a different kind of group," Mo told him.

"Oh. I see. Right. Well, please. No one stand on formality on my account. We're all equals here, right?"

"Equally cursed," Jodi grumbled into her mostly empty coffee cup.

"Right, it's a little past time for the meeting to begin," Kitty said. "Who wants to start?"

It was Jodi, of course. As curious as Kitty was about the new man on the far side of the circle, she first had to listen to Jodi's woes about ordering coffee for the better part of an hour.

But Wil, bless his heart, pushed back at Jodi in a way that Kitty had never had the courage to. What was so wrong with plain black coffee, anyway? And if she wanted something fancier, couldn't she get what she needed to make it at home? Had she even *tried* remembering what she liked when she wasn't standing at the counter with ten people waiting behind her and at least two baristas waiting in front of her?

"I want what I want, when I want it, and I want someone else to make it for me!" Jodi finally burst out. "What part of that is so very hard to understand?"

"Well, it just seems to me, in your case, Mr. Samson's curse didn't even fix the problem," he said.

"What do you mean?" Jodi growled at him.

His cheeks were flushed with embarrassment, but he pressed on. "Well, he cursed you to only order the simplest thing on the menu because he didn't want you to hold up the line. But it sounds like you're still holding up lines, trying to force out words that won't come. Actually, I think he made the problem worse."

Jodi blustered out a series of sounds that weren't really words, unless they were too many words trying to be spoken all at once. Then she got up, snatched her coat down from its peg, and stormed out of the cellar.

"I'm sorry. I feel like I've crossed a line," Wil said.

"The only thing you said that was wrong was calling him 'Mr. Samson'," Mo said as he chewed the last of his Danish. "Around here, we call him That Bastard Magician Samson, and nothing else."

The new man barked out a laugh that he quickly smothered with a hand over his mouth.

"I have to catch the train back to the suburbs," Wil said, glancing at his watch.

"You don't even live in the Hidden City?" Kitty asked.

"No. Never had much use for magic, not even arithmancy. Ironic. I was just visiting my mother when That Bastard Magician Samson and I crossed paths," he said. Then he grinned. Clearly, he liked that name for his oppressor much better.

"We meet every week. I hope you'll stop by again," Kitty said.

"Plan to," he said.

And then he was gone, and Kitty, Lara and Mo were alone with the man who still hadn't told them his name.

"Nice meeting. Like the concept," the man said. "I had no idea these groups even existed. Can you believe that?"

"No offense, but you've never even told us who you are," Mo said.

"Sorry. I'm Myke Fuller. The first man cursed by… what did you call him? Oh, yes. That Bastard Magician Samson."

"How could you possibly know you were the first?" Mo said. "I mean, I always assumed that was me. I ferried him in my boat through the underground canal system from where he had stolen the Rod of Circe to his sanctum sanctorum. Which was tricky to find for any escort, I don't care what he said the other escorts told him. Now, because he couldn't get to where he wanted to go, I can't either. Ever. But he didn't quite seem to know how the rod even worked when he cursed me."

"I don't think he quite knew with me either," Myke allowed with a nod of his head. "But I know I was the first. Because he cursed me the instant after he stole the Rod of Circe from me."

"That was your magic?" Kitty asked. Lara was flailing her hands excitedly, and Kitty guessed if it was possible for them to both speak in unison, they would've been.

"I didn't create the Rod of Circe. It was a family heirloom," Myke said.

"What kind of family creates an object like that?" Kitty demanded. She gave up all pretense of sitting now, too keyed up for the focus even just squatting demanded. She preferred to stand with her feet planted. But Myke stood up, too. Even without the elaborate robes that went with those facial tattoos, he radiated power.

"So, what's your curse?" Mo asked.

"The Fuller family is one of the oldest in the New World. As are all of yours, coincidentally," he said.

"You researched us?" Kitty asked.

"I have done more research on all of this than you could possibly imagine," he said, almost a challenge.

But Mo scoffed. "She owns a bookshop that doesn't make anything like a profit. All so she can read anything she can get her hands on. And you're going to impress her with doing a little research?"

"Yes," Myke said, giving Mo an amused glance. But then he looked down at Kitty again. "Everything you can get your hands on?" He raised an eyebrow at her.

"I can muster enough focus to turn the pages," Kitty said, crossing her arms defensively. But she deflated a little as she was forced to admit," I get customers to set the books out for me on a table in the back. Once the covers are open, I can turn the pages on my own. Twenty open at a time usually keeps me in reading material until another customer happens by."

"Usually," Myke repeated, not a question. "Did you know you were the third person he cursed? After Mo and me?"

"I did not," Kitty admitted. But Lara was waving her hand to get his attention.

"Yes, Lara Tilley. You were the fourth," he said with a smile. "Talked his ear off, did you? At first, I thought you must've spilled some dire secret of his, but after years of searching for that secret, I've concluded it was just the volume of words he objected to. Am I correct?"

Lara nodded as she gave him a chagrined little smile. Then she held up two fingers and turned them back and forth.

"In both senses of the word 'volume', I'm guessing?" he said, and her grin widened. "Not remotely sorry, are you? I mean, curse aside, if you had your voice back, you'd do it again?"

She nodded, more emphatically this time.

"Can we get back to this family heirloom of yours?" Mo asked. "And why you're here?"

"And what your curse is?" Kitty put in.

"Well, they're all related," Myke said. "Short version is, the Rod of Circe was in my family for generations, back in the day. It disappeared for the last four generations, believed lost or possibly even destroyed. Ever since I was a kid, I was obsessed with finding the thing. It had to be in one of the family properties, somewhere. The enchanted tower back in England that lurks unseen by mundane eyes deep in the hills of the north country. The family townhouse in the magical quarter of Old Amsterdam. Perhaps even here, in our newest home in the Hidden City interwoven throughout Minneapolis."

"Which one was it?" Kitty asked.

"Here," Myke said. "Just where great-great-granddad dropped it, in the cave under our home on Boom Island."

"Is the name just a coincidence?" Kitty asked.

"Boom Island? I have no idea. Nothing's gone boom there in my lifetime."

"I meant the Rod of Circe."

"Oh, no. It really is the very wand that once turned Odysseus' men into pigs. She's a very old spirit, that rod. She's mellowed since then," he said with a wistful fondness in his eyes.

"Has she?" Mo asked pointedly. "Kitty can't touch anything, and Lara can't talk. I can't get anywhere I want to go. I'm not really sure any of that is 'mellower' than being a pig."

"I think it is," Kitty whispered to him, and Lara nodded her agreement.

"I'm getting off track here," Myke said. He checked off fingers, "family heirloom. Personal obsession. Found it under the house. Oh, right. Samson."

"Where does he enter into the picture?" Kitty asked.

"Elliot Samson, as he was called when I knew him, was a classmate of mine at the magical academies. We went to the same magical grammar school, which was tedious enough. He always had to have the desk next to mine, always had to be part of whatever I was doing at recess, that kind of thing. Then he followed me to the same prep school designed for those looking to pursue ceremonial magic as a vocation."

"Followed you? Like, on purpose?" Kitty asked.

"Believe me, he had no calling," Myke said. "He's a terrible magician."

"But..." Kitty said, gesturing to herself and Mo and Lara on either side of her.

"That was only possible because he took my rod," Myke said.

"Because he knew you were looking for it?" Mo asked.

"He stayed close by my side just in case I *should* find it," Myke said. "All through prep school, which he barely passed. Even when I went to England for my higher-level studies. Somehow he finagled a way into the same program, a program he wasn't remotely qualified for."

"Did he graduate?" Mo asked. "I mean, I saw him in my ferry when he had your rod. He didn't have the tattoos."

"No, he didn't graduate," Myke said. "I don't know what he did or where he was. Not for the eight years after he flunked out of the school in England. I thought I was well shut of him, that he was out of my life forever. I finished my studies. I interned in China for a year. A very prestigious assignment, but not really my thing. Ceremonial magic is very, very dry. Trust me.

"So, I came back home and resumed my search for the rod. Never knowing that the entire time, Samson was still watching me. Somehow, he knew. The minute I found that rod, he knew."

"But how did he take it from you?" Kitty asked. "Even if you stopped pursuing ceremonial magic as a vocation, just passing the program makes you more adept at magic than almost anyone. Doesn't it?"

"Yes, thank you. It does," he said. "All I can say is, I was careless. I didn't think much of Samson. And, of course, I didn't know anyone else even knew the rod was in my possession. I hadn't told my own father. There hadn't been any time. And yet, Samson knew. He came to my house on the pretense of just visiting while in town, and I foolishly let him in. And while I was making coffee for the two of us, he went up to my study and snatched the rod right out of the innermost secret drawer of my writing desk."

"That's crazy," Mo said, shaking his head.

"It happened," Myke said with a shrug. "He came down to the kitchen, but not to gloat so much as to be sure I could never take the rod back from him."

"That's your curse?" Kitty guessed.

"He was pretty specific," Myke said. "I can't take the rod back myself. I can't build a machine to take the rod back for me. I can't use any magic known or unknown to humankind to take the rod back for me. I can't pay anyone to take the rod back."

He paused, eyebrows raised expectantly. After a few seconds, Mo started to chuckle.

"I don't get it," Kitty said. "If you came here for help, doesn't that rule us out?"

"Not if he doesn't pay us," Mo told her, and Myke nodded.

"But that's a huge loophole," Kitty said. "It can't be that hard to find volunteers. Especially lately. In another year, the challenge will be to find someone he *hasn't* cursed."

But Lara was shaking her head, gesturing with her hands as if hastily erasing a chalkboard. Then she pointed at Myke, then Mo, then Kitty, then Lara.

"She gets it," Myke said.

"We're the first four," Kitty said. "How does that matter?"

"Because the Rod of Circe exchanges magic with her companion human," Myke said. "Now, that companion is That Bastard Magician Samson. Hence the petty, unimaginative curses. Like any of us needed to endure an hour of why a venti americano is just *not* the thing."

"But he was the one with the rod with all of us too," Kitty said. "Are you saying some of you lingered in the rod or something?" She scrunched up her nose in confusion. She ran a magic bookshop, but that mostly ran to unreliable divination texts and the occasional rhyming charm of small effect. She could use a little magic, but even with all her reading, she didn't really understand how it worked, anymore than she understood quantum physics.

But Myke had been a ceremonial magician. If half the rumors were true about the power those magicians held, he was not to be trifled with. And would certainly know more than she did about how all this worked.

"I had a rapport with her," Myke said. There was a wistful look to his face, his eyes unfocused as if seeing only the past and not the world around him in the present. "Some of that rapport lingered, especially through the first few curses. It's not my magic, not any part of me. It was just a lingering sense in her of the things I had talked with her about, in our very short time together."

"I don't get it," Kitty said, throwing up her hands.

Myke blinked as if suddenly awake and looked around at the three of them gazing anxiously at him, waiting for him to explain.

"She had a sense of humor," he said. "Turning Odyssey's men into pigs? Come on. That's spot-on irony. Maybe even too on the nose."

"I don't find my own situation particularly funny," Mo said. "Ironic, maybe. In an Alanis Morissette kind of way."

Lara scowled at him, but Kitty wasn't in the mood for a half-pantomime discussion of pop song lyrics.

"Whether those sailors had it coming or not, we didn't," Kitty said.

"Agreed, with the possible exception of me," Myke said. "Not that I deserved it. But taking me out was necessary for him to keep the rod. So it makes sense. The rest of you? Not so much. You've named him well; he really is just a petty bastard."

Lara snapped her fingers to get everyone's attention, then held up a page of her leather-bound journal. And Kitty realized she had not been scowling over the meaning of the word 'irony.' She had put together what Mo had been missing.

In a neat script that didn't show a hint of how rushed its execution had been, Lara had written, "the Rod of Circe wants to be with Myke, not with Samson. The curses all have big loopholes by design."

"Exactly," Myke said, then gave a nervous laugh. "Good work, Lara. It took me *years* to figure that out. But that's why I'm here now. The four of us, we're the only ones who can stop this. We can take down Samson."

"By taking the rod from him?" Mo asked. "Is he also keeping it in a secret drawer in a writing desk?"

"Probably not anything so easy," Myke admitted.

"Can we reverse the curses?" Kitty asked, all in a rush.

"That, I don't know. But with the rod, I promise to try," he said.

"So, what do we do now?" Mo asked. "Do you know where his sanctum sanctorum is?"

"No, but you do," Myke said.

Mo blew out a long sigh. "Do I need to explain my curse again?"

"No. You were quite clear," Myke said.

"Because just because I've been there once doesn't mean I can find it again. Kind of the opposite, in fact. And it's not a matter of focus. Kitty told me how she can focus to touch things years ago, and I tried to do the same to defeat my own curse. I really tried. I've studied with Taoist masters, trying to learn how to let go of wanting things. Few have worked harder at wu wei than I have. But it's part of the curse, I guess. I can't rid myself of wanting."

"I want to have a longer conversation with you about what you learned, for sure. But in the meantime, I just need you to get us to That Bastard Magician Samson's sanctum sanctorum," Myke said, as if it were the most reasonable request in the world.

Then Mo did something Kitty had never seen him do before. He got angry. "Do you think I haven't tried to get back there? Like a thousand times? There is literally nowhere I want to be more than where he is, so I can take a run at him."

Myke gave him a slow grin. Then Lara was grinning too, and Kitty realized she was a step behind her yet again.

Then it hit her. "Oh," she said, startled.

Mo turned to her, but his anger had vanished as suddenly as it had appeared. "What, Kitty?" he asked.

"I think the plan is for you to focus on how much you want to get to Samson," she said slowly, but when Myke and Lara nodded along, she gained confidence. "Focus on wanting to get to him, but ferry us through the underground canals to where you dropped him off. And when we get there, he won't be home."

"Easier to burgle than to rob," Myke said.

"But I thought this was a revenge thing," Mo said.

"Once I have the rod back in my possession, I'll help you get all the revenge you could ever want," Myke promised.

Mo blew out another long breath, then chuckled as he shrugged. "What the hell. Let's give it a shot."

"How do we get to your ferry?" Kitty asked. She could hear the driving rain, even down in the cellar. She didn't fancy walking through that. Even noncorporeal as she was, she still felt things passing through her, and it wasn't pleasant.

Mo looked around the cellar as if seeing it for the first time. Kitty knew for a fact there was no other way out than the stairs they had all come down. There weren't even any windows.

But, being an escort through the secret ways of the Hidden City, his magic was second only to Myke's in that cellar just then. So Kitty wasn't entirely surprised when he nodded in satisfaction to himself then crossed the room to slip into the shadows under the stairs. She heard him shifting her extra chairs aside. Then he called back, "well, come on if you're coming on."

Myke followed first, then Lara. It wasn't until the two of them suddenly disappeared from her sight that she realized what Mo had found. There was a trapdoor under her stairs, an old Prohibition era sneak hole that led down to the sewers. And all the sewers led to the river, one way or another.

But there wasn't a stairway down. There was a ladder. Her working relationship with floors made the steps of a staircase doable, but the rungs of a ladder?

She had never tried. She would almost rather try walking in the rain. As hideous as the feeling of water constantly falling through her was, at least there would be solid ground under her feet.

"Kitty?" Myke called up to her from some point in the darkness far below the trapdoor, far below even the point where the light from the open door reached.

Kitty focused every bit of attention she could muster, which took longer than normal because her heart refused to stop racing with excitement. But shifting her attention to the rhythmic sound of the rain finally allowed her to become solid enough for long enough to climb down those rusted iron rungs, down to the slick stone of the sewer below.

The others were standing at the edge of a sort of quay, and Mo was holding a lantern Kitty had never seen before. It hung from a chain in his hand, but the art deco design of it had no place in a sewer. If anything, it looked like he'd ripped it out of a fixture in the Foshay Tower. The metal parts were rusted, but the glass was intact, and it glowed with a greenish, magical light.

"The water is high!" Mo yelled back over his shoulder as he leaned far out over the rushing water, holding the lantern at arm's length upstream. The green light of the lantern made the normally brown water look inky black and slick, more like oil than water. But it was moving dizzyingly fast, the roar of it echoing off the brick walls of the sewer around them almost too loud for her to hear Mo's words when he shouted, "Look, there she is! There's my baby!"

A gondola—one that looked more like Captain Nemo's *Nautilus* at Disney World than anything that floated in the canals of Venice—bobbed over the current towards them, coming to a rest at the quay despite the rush of water against its hull. Mo hung the lantern from a pole in the stern then reached out with both hands to help Myke and Lara on board.

But there was no help for Kitty, who lingered uncertainly on the solid stone of the quay, her heart in her throat.

She had never tried standing on a boat before. What if it was less like a floor and more like a chair? What if she fell right through it? If she ended up standing at the bottom of the sewer itself, the water was surely taller than her head. She'd never get out.

And all that water would be moving through her. Just the thought of that, so much worse than rain, almost had her running back to the rungs, back up to her nice, safe bookshop.

"We need you, Kitty," Myke said, as if hearing her thoughts. For all she knew, he could. She had no idea what the limits of a ceremonial magician's powers were.

Lara gestured for her to join them, and something in the imploring expression on her face made Kitty certain that if she did fall through the boat, none of them would abandon her.

She jumped.

Not only was the bottom of the boat solid under her feet, it wasn't even unsteady. The water sloshed against its sides, but it remained motionless and level.

Lara gestured again for Kitty to sit on the bench beside her, and Kitty sank down in her usual fake-sitting squat. Lara's hands fluttered around her, part in a desperate desire to communicate with her, part in an equally desperate desire to give Kitty a happy hug or at least squeeze her hand.

Kitty felt a stab of sadness. Lara was really her best friend, she realized. And they had never touched, no matter how badly one or the other of them had needed a hug at support group meetings. And they had never really had a chat together.

Kitty really hoped that Myke could undo the curses. For all their sakes.

"Let's go get that bastard," Myke said to Mo, who laughed, then took up his pole to push them away from the quay. He drove the pole down hard and pivoted the entire ferry around until they were facing upstream. Then the boat propelled itself over the water, only occasionally guided by Mo's gentle hand at the pole.

The only time the ride became even slightly uncomfortable was the three times they had to launch up and over a waterfall, and only then because they had to squat low to avoid hitting their heads against the stone arches that supported the roof above.

The further they traveled, the calmer the water became until Mo drove his pole down to the bottom again to force the boat to another halt. There was no quay here, but when Kitty looked up, she saw the bottom of a sewer tunnel above them. The lowest rungs of the ladder were just in reach.

"This is it," Mo said, as if he barely dared to believe the truth of his own words. "This is it. At last."

"Kitty, can you handle the climb?" Myke asked. "It could be a long one."

"I'll manage," she said. There was no way she was failing now, not when they were all so close.

She jumped first, caught the bottom rung in her hands, and started to climb. Usually, she couldn't really feel what she was touching. It was like she was wearing thick gloves under wool mittens, only getting a sense of pressure with no tactile sensations at all. But as she climbed, she could swear she was feeling the cold of the iron, the slick dampness of it, the abrasive quality of the rust that was eating away at it.

Then the tunnel ended, completely closed off by a heavy access cover. She could see rain pattering through a hole in its exact center. But there was no way she could shift it.

"You'll have to pass through," Myke called up to her, reading her mind again.

"I've never tried that before," Kitty said. She had walked through walls before, but that was different. The ground was always there for her. But the rung she clung to, what would happen if she tried ghosting through the cover? Would she ghost through the rung as well? Would she fall?

"Wu wei," Mo called up to her.

"You've spent years learning that," Kitty called back to him. "You want me to get it in a hot minute?"

"Don't try to do it, just do it," he said, as if that were the simplest thing in the world.

Well, maybe it was.

Kitty launched herself off the top rung. She felt that cold iron pass through her.

Then she was lying on wet grass. Miserably, coldly wet grass.

It felt glorious.

"Now you need to grasp this," she could just hear Myke saying. She rolled onto her side to see some sort of metal tool thrusting up through the hole in the center of the cover.

"Grasping it is one thing," she said even as she got to her feet.

"The weight of this lid is nothing compared to the focus you need to touch things at all," Myke said. "Trust me. I've studied this."

"If you say so," Kitty said. She squatted as low as she could while still having her feet on either side of the mouth of the access way. Then she closed her hands over the haft of the tool.

It was delightful, how much she was feeling today. Cold iron, mostly, and colder rain. But she couldn't wait to get inside this sanctum sanctorum. She was going to touch all the things.

Then she lifted. The muscles in her thighs screamed in protest, nothing compared to how badly the muscles in her hands wanted to give up and let the tool slip out of their grasp. But she could hear a grinding sound, and she knew she wasn't exerting herself in vain.

She pulled harder. She couldn't lift the lid out of its resting place entirely, but she shifted it enough for Myke to put a shoulder against it and heave it the rest of the way clear.

Then they were all sprawled out on the grass, gasping up into the rain-filled sky.

Lara sat up first, looking around in mild curiosity. Then she saw something that excited her and she started slapping at all of them—save, of course, Kitty—pointing up towards something. They turned to look.

They were lying on the grass at the bottom of a hill, in a park with scattered picnic tables and lots of trees. But rising up over the treetops was a water tower, white concrete topped by a distinctive green-tiled conical roof that flared out like the brim of a hat over windows that offered a panoramic view from the open space on top of the water tank.

"I know where we are," Kitty said. "That's the Witch's Hat. We're in Prospect Park. *This* is where he lives?"

"Cursing people is surprisingly lucrative," Mo said. "The homes around here are not cheap."

"Which house is his?" Kitty wondered. But Lara shook her head at her, then pointed again at the former water tower, now protected local landmark. Specifically, at the witch's hat top of it.

"I think she's right," Myke said, squinting through the rain. "There is definitely something up there."

Kitty didn't see anything, but so far trusting Myke had been working out. When he started climbing the steep hill up to the base of the tower, she followed without question. And so did Mo and Lara.

The door at the bottom of the tower was unsurprisingly padlocked, but Myke touched a glowing fingertip to it with a few whispered words of power, and the lock fell open of its own accord.

"Still not sure you needed us," Kitty said as they climbed the stairs that spiraled around the central tank of the dark interior.

"I do," Myke assured her. "That lock was quite mundane, to keep the locals out of the tower. The locks ahead that bar us from Samson's sanctum sanctorum will be another matter entirely."

The stairs ended in an open space, concrete floor below with wood-tiled conical cap above. Despite the waist-high walls all around, the wind blew coldly through the eight large windows, bringing the rain with it. Kitty went to the edge, to look down at the treetops below. She could only imagine how breathtaking the view would be on a day with nicer weather. Or when the trees were bare of leaves and everything was covered with snow.

"Here, everyone. Lara's found it," Myke said, and Kitty turned to see Lara holding the end of a rope. Kitty followed the rope with her eyes up into the cap of the tower, but it ended in midair, not attached to anything visible.

Lara gave the rope a tug, and a voice boomed all around them. "Speak, friend, and enter," it intoned.

"Great, so I'm not the only one Samson has ripped off," Myke grumbled under his breath.

"Well, at least we know what to say," Mo said brightly.

"No, that's not it," Myke said, then nodded at Lara to give the rope another pull. The same voice spoke the same phrase, but something about Myke's frown told Kitty he had noticed something she had missed.

"That's his voice, isn't it?" Mo said.

"Yes. That was Samson," Myke agreed. "Samson, who has no friends."

"So what does it mean?" Kitty asked.

"This is the rod's doing, we know that," Myke said, pacing as he thought it through. "She created this magic lock for him, at his request but for her own purpose. We hold the key, if only we can figure out how."

"So the rod chose his voice to speak? To flatter his vanity?" Kitty said.

"I think it's important, what you said," Mo said, looking at Myke, who had stopped pacing. "He has no friends. So who does he expect to answer?"

"The same as asked. Himself," Myke said drily.

"But we have the key," Kitty said, hoping speaking the words aloud would shake the answer loose. But she had nothing.

Then Myke turned on his heel and charged almost aggressively up to where Lara was still holding the rope. She flinched involuntarily, but then looked up at him expectantly.

And he was grinning at her again.

"He took your voice from you," he said to her in a feverish excitement. "*Your* voice."

She nodded, eyes bright, equally excited but clearly not quite following his logic yet.

"But I bet you're one hell of a mimic. Yes?" he prompted.

Lara grinned, then pulled the rope again. This time, when the voice intoned, "speak, friend, and enter," she answered in the same pretentiously deep voice, "friend."

And suddenly Kitty could see the whole length of rope, and the bottom of a floating castle.

And the open well protruding down through its stone floor, from which the rope dangled.

The feel of the rope was lovely, untouched by rain. It wasn't coarse like twine or cord. It was silk, braided thick but still soft under her grasp. She actually enjoyed the climb.

Then they were in a room that, despite being all rose-colored marble threaded through with veins of gold, gave Kitty the overwhelming impression of being a mudroom. Well, every proper Minnesotan home had one of those. Even the floating castles, apparently.

"What now?" she asked eagerly. "I suppose Mo, Lara and I have each done our part, so it's up to you?"

"No, not me," Myke said. "The curse still holds me. I can take no action. No, I think it's you who's up again, Kitty. But I can guide us through the castle. I can feel the rod. She's calling to me."

"He really left her behind?" Mo said. "He's out in the world without her? What if he wants to curse someone?"

"He'll be back here in an instant to fetch her," Myke said grimly. "We don't have much time. Quick, up these stairs. His sanctum sanctorum will be in the highest room of the highest tower. Because of course it will."

Running up endless flights of stairs was exhausting work, especially after all the climbing they had already done. But even as she fought to keep breathing, Kitty could feel the grin that just wouldn't leave her face.

She hadn't had this much fun in ages. And to think, when she started the support group, she had only wanted to just not be sad all the time.

Funny how things worked out.

The stairs finally ended in a room much like the top of the Witch's Hat Water Tower, only with much higher views and a good deal less wind. Which was a good thing, since the space was filled with desks and tables, all covered in books, scrolls, and great quantities of loose paper. There were no windows around them, just open air on all sides. One little breeze would send all that paper out into the clouds around them, never to be seen again.

"He really can control the weather," Lara said in her Samson voice, and Kitty laughed.

"Boy, as good as it is to hear your thoughts, I really hope we get your proper voice back," she said.

"Not as much as I do," Lara/Samson said.

"Kitty, I need you one last time," Myke called from the far side of the room. Kitty made her way over to find him standing over a desk he had apparently just swept clean of all its clutter. He was chuckling drily.

"What is it?" she asked.

"It's my desk," Myke said. "Literally, it's an exact copy of my desk."

"So you know how to get in," Mo said as he ran his fingertips over the woodwork, feeling for the catches for hidden drawers.

"I do," Myke said.

"I know you can't open them yourself, but you can tell me, right?" Mo said.

"I could," Myke conceded, "or Kitty could just—"

Kitty didn't even wait for him to finish his thought. She just thrust her hand inside the desk.

It should've been harder than jumping through the lid to get out of the sewer, really. Grasping an object and pulling it through another object. She wasn't even sure it should be possible.

And yet she acted without thinking. But the rod told her it would be fine. The second her fingers brushed against it, she could hear the voice in her head telling her so. The rod wanted to go with her, to let Kitty hand her to Myke.

And so she did, in one smooth motion.

"Wu wei," Kitty said to Mo, and he nodded appreciatively back to her.

"It's her. It's really her," Myke said, running his fingers over the rod, turning it over and over in his hands. "I almost can't believe it. But I have her back."

The other three watched this mostly silent reunion play out for what felt like forever. Then Lara caught Kitty and Mo by their sleeves, pulling them to the far side of the room. Kitty thought at first this was to give Myke and the rod some privacy.

But then Lara said in her Samson voice, "please tell me I'm not the only one who thought this rod was going to turn into a woman when we got here?"

"Thank you!" Kitty breathed.

"I totally got a 'the rod is my girlfriend' vibe off this guy the whole time," Mo agreed.

They all laughed, but all too briefly.

"Still cursed," Lara said in her Samson voice.

"Still cursed," Kitty agreed, swiping her ghostly hand through a nearby table.

"I have a feeling I'm still cursed as well," Mo said.

"Such little faith!" Myke said, suddenly back among them. He had the rod in his hands, his fingertips constantly running over it like he could never get enough of touching its smooth bronze surface. But then he checked himself with a little click of his tongue and turned his hands palms-up, the rod resting across them. Then he thrust his hands towards them, as if presenting the rod to them.

Kitty wasn't the only one to recoil. The way the light in her bookshop had reflected along that bronze length in that last moment before her life had changed forever still haunted her. A single image she could never erase from her mind.

"Just touch it," Myke said, thrusting the rod towards Mo.

Mo chewed viciously at his lip, but then blew out a breath before reaching out with a single fingertip to tap the side of the rod. He retracted his hand at once, clutching it close to his chest as if he'd just accidentally touched a hot stove.

But a slow grin spread across his face, becoming a wide smile that he turned on Kitty and Lara.

"It worked. I don't know how I know, I just know. Touch it!" he said, gesturing for Kitty to go next.

But Lara needed no prompting. She lunged at Myke, pressing both her palms down on the length of the rod. There was a sound like the ringing of a bell, although whether it was real or just in her head the way she had heard the rod talking to her before, Kitty couldn't be sure.

But there was no doubt the happy laughter bubbling out of Lara was totally a hundred percent real.

"It worked!" she said. "It really worked!"

Her voice was deeper than Kitty had ever imagined it would be, slow and sultry even in her excitement. The sort of voice most people would gladly listen to read a phone book or the ingredients off a soda can.

That Bastard Magician Samson really was a bastard, taking that voice away.

"Your turn, Kitty," Lara said, and Myke held out the rod for her.

Kitty traded a grin with Lara, then another with Mo. Then she reached out to touch the rod.

And her hand went right through it, as ghostly as ever.

She was too stunned for thought, too stunned even to hear more than the murmur of Lara's worried voice, Mo's reassuring tones.

But she heard Myke when she said, distinctly and in a voice just sort of magically commanding, "try again."

Kitty reached out again, but her hand hovered over the rod on Myke's palms, unwilling to try again. Or, rather, to fail again.

But the rod's voice was in her head again, promising her it would be all right. She just needed to move slowly. Move with focus. Move with intent.

Kitty closed her eyes. Then she lowered her hand, fully expecting to feel nothing at all.

But then the coolness of the bronze touched her palm, then the warmth of Myke's upraised hands. Before she even dared open her eyes, Lara's arms were around her, and then Mo's as well.

"There we all go," Myke said, tucking the rod tucked securely in a little custom-made sheath at his belt that Kitty had definitely not noticed before. "Of course we're not done yet."

"We're not?" Lara asked, still hugging Kitty.

"Four curses broken, how many more to go?" he said.

"Hundreds," Mo guessed.

"Thousands, actually," Kitty corrected him.

"That we know of," Lara added.

"Don't get discouraged," Myke said cheerfully. "We're the perfect team, really." He pointed at Kitty and said, "You, with your focus and intent." Then he pointed at Mo, "You, with your wu wei." And then Lara: "And you, with your flexibility. I think in the end we'll all find this curse business was a net good, bringing us all together like it has."

"But what about Samson?" Kitty asked.

"Without the rod, he's nothing," Myke said, his tone as close to coming angry as Kitty had ever heard it.

But then he broke his own sour mood with a sudden laugh. "Come on. Let's get out of here before That Bastard Magician Samson realizes he's just That Bastard Samson."

WINTER'S END

Once, on one of our early anniversaries, my husband and I had gone to Iceland for a long weekend. We soaked in the waters of the Blue Lagoon, sat up late each night hoping for a glimpse of the Northern Lights, and even taken a day trip to explore ice caves on top of one of the glaciers.

That trip was when I had first learned about ice cleats. Walking on a glacier, especially in the caves with many chutes down to oblivion that are barely roped off from the main path, they were a lifesaver.

I just never expected to need them just to check my mail.

Or to stay upright while shoveling yet another fresh six inches of snow off the pack of hard ice that never relinquished its hold on my driveway. Especially not the bottom hundred and fifty feet, the part that ran from the dirt road, under the thick if currently bare branches of all our many trees, and over the culvert that in the spring would be a roaring stream of rushing water.

I was the one who wanted to move back to Minnesota, the magical world of my early childhood I had left behind midway through kindergarten and had never been back to. But my husband had been totally on board. He was ready for a change, too.

And when we had been house-shopping, I had been the one who

had fallen in love with it at first sight. I freely admit that. But after a decade living in a townhouse in D.C. with the bustling sidewalk of a busy street right outside our front windows, the idea of living in a house set so far back from the road it couldn't even be seen through the trees had felt absolutely magical.

It still was, I reminded myself as I took a break from my shoveling to look up the hill to where my house stood, looking pretty modest from this angle. But the basement was a walkout to a cute little patio, and the main floor offered an amazing view of a stretch of wetlands that, unlike most of the open fields around our new home, would never, ever be developed into a planned community of "pick one of our five options" build-to-suit homes.

But three hundred feet of driveway was a lot. Especially when the snowblower purchased new the fall before had yet to actually fire up when she attempted to start it.

I was still gazing up at my house when I heard the crunch of tires over snow and turned to see the post office truck pulling away from my mailbox. I had almost finished shoveling the driveway, after a mere three hours, but what remained was the worst of it. The heavy boulders of dirty ice the snowplows shoved into my driveway, forming an all but impassable wall.

It was like they did it on purpose.

And my back was already killing me.

Every time I'd swear to myself that next time I'd start at the bottom and work my way up. But every time it snowed, I'd open the garage door, shovel in hand, and just start working on the snow that was closest.

Well, it wasn't like I was going anywhere. With our only car still with my husband in D.C., I was basically stuck at home all the time. Thanks to the internet, I had been working from home for years, but this always being home was quite different. We hadn't even thought of it as a problem to be solved when we'd bought the house. We were both so thoroughly city people, it hadn't occurred to us that in most of the country, if you didn't have a car you were out of luck. There was no public transportation to speak of, and absolutely nothing was within walking distance.

If I were really desperate, I could summon a car with a rideshare app. But shoveling and attempting to deice the driveway was eating into all my free time, anyway. I didn't have the time to go anywhere.

And at the moment, I really didn't have the time to start tackling those boulders of ice. I would be punching in for my shift in less than an hour, and even if no one else would be around to smell me, I really wanted a shower first.

I leaned the shovel against the nearest snowbank—taller than shoulder-height on me now, which was a big contributing factor to the stiffness in my back, all that throwing—and headed out to the mailbox.

The minute I opened the door and saw the little orange card, I felt a rush of annoyance that was starting to edge into actual anger. Another redelivery card. I snatched it out into the sunlight and glared at the box checked. *Sorry we missed you!*

"Sorry you missed me," I grumbled to myself. "You didn't miss me. You can't possibly miss me. I'm always right here."

I guess there's no box on the form to check that says anything like, "I didn't trust my driving or walking skills to get me up your drive-way." But they clearly needed one. They hadn't *missed* me.

It was doubly annoying considering I had been standing in the driveway at the time. He could've shouted for me to come take the damn box. There was no way he didn't see me. Not in my bright orange parka.

I looked in the mailbox, but there was nothing but the card. The card with redelivery directions that I knew from months of experience was not going to end with me getting my mail. Not without getting to the post office myself to pick it up.

It was an hour and a half's walk away. In good weather. Which this was not.

I was squinting at the card, trying to figure out who could've sent this package and determine whether it was worth taking a rideshare to the post office to pick it up, when the grinding of tires on snow right behind me had me scurrying back to my own driveway.

But the tires followed me. I fought my way through the protective wall of ice to where I had left my shovel, but I heard the crunch of a plow biting into the boulders of ice behind me and turned to see what I should've expected.

It was my neighbor Oskar, the only one of my neighbors I had yet met after nearly a year of living in the house. Or, perhaps I should say it was my neighbor's Bobcat with the plow attachment, digging into the city plow's ice wall at an angle. When he'd finally broken through, he worked off a chunk of the wall and shoved it all the way across the road, to the alfalfa field on the far side. He shoved it far off the road, driving his little vehicle expertly over the uneven ground.

I was pretty sure if it had been me, I would've rolled the thing. Then again, I wouldn't be trying to push everything so far off the road.

Oskar has this thing about keeping the snow flat. It's very important to him not to pile it up. I don't know if this is a flooding in the spring worry or mere aesthetics or what. I just know he feels pretty strongly about it.

Maybe it's why he owns his own Bobcat.

He had to make a number of passes, but in the end he still did in under ten minutes what it would've taken me the better part of an hour to do, and far less painfully.

He usually just waves and leaves without a word when he does this, but this time he actually parked the Bobcat and got out to talk to me.

Which was always an interesting experience.

"Thanks so much, Oskar," I said. "I was just running out of steam myself and was going to leave the rest until tomorrow."

He didn't answer right away, just looked down at the ice we were both standing on. It was so thick you couldn't even see the surface of the driveway beneath it. Nothing but yellowish, brownish ice stained by the runoff from the dirt road we both lived on. Now that I had taken the top layer of snow off, it was starting to gleam like a hockey rink once again.

Then he looked up at me again and said, "your husband was here last week."

"Yes, for spring break," I said. Not that it looked remotely like spring where we were standing. But even the local kids had had the week off school for spring break, snow or no snow.

Of course, back in D.C., it really was spring. The cherry blossoms were about to start blooming, or so my husband had told me.

I hated the weather in D.C. I really hated it. I had lived there for most of the last thirty years of my life, but I had never stopped hating the smothering, humid, swamp heat of the place. Even standing in all the snow and on top of the ice that just might be the death of me, I still preferred where I was to where I had been.

But I did regret missing seeing the cherry blossoms bloom.

Oskar was just looking at me, and I belatedly realized that I had yet again mistaken what sounded like a mere statement to actually be a question in disguise.

He wasn't telling me my husband had been home last week. We both knew that was true; what would be the point in saying it?

No, what he was doing, in his backwards sort of way, was asking me why, if my husband had been home the week before, was my snowblower apparently still broken?

"Mike looked at the snow blower while he was here," I assured him. "One of the parts is bad. So I guess that's good. It wasn't my fault that I couldn't get it started. That's always good to know, right?" I gave a little laugh, but Oskar just slow-blinked at me. "Anyway, he ordered the part, but it's on back-order until June."

Because of course it is.

"But I don't mind shoveling, really. It's good cardio, right?"

I was such a bad liar.

But Oskar wasn't looking at me. He was looking at the snowbanks that lined my driveway. The ones that were taller than my shoulders. One more snowfall and I'd have nowhere to put the snow. I don't think I can throw shovelfuls over a wall taller than my head.

"It has to be spring soon, right?" I finished lamely.

Oskar just sighed and walked back to his Bobcat. He fired it up and puttered back up the road to where his own house lay, so far back from the road I could only make out the outline of his roof, and then only in the winter when the trees were bare.

I hefted the snow shovel onto my shoulder and made my way step by carefully planted step up the driveway to the open door of my garage.

It was hard to guess what Oskar was thinking, aside from a general disapproval of the height of my snowbanks. When we'd first moved into the house, almost exactly a year ago to the date in the heart of an unseasonably early spring, the first thing he'd said to Mike and I after we'd introduced ourselves was, "the previous owners were Socialists."

Then he'd given us one of his penetrating looks.

We had stumbled out of that conversation, but later that evening in the middle of some mildly entertaining movie we were streaming, I had gasped aloud. At Mike's raised eyebrow, I had said, "he was trying to ask us how we voted, wasn't he?"

"Was he?" Mike asked skeptically. Then he blew out an irritated breath. "It's not remotely any of his business."

"Maybe he just thinks all schoolteachers are socialists or something?" I had guessed.

"We're not that far out in the sticks," Mike laughed. "Besides, he already knows I'm a university professor, not a *schoolteacher*."

I wasn't sure Oskar would see the difference, but I knew better than to say so out loud.

And after a few months in the house together, Mike had had to go back to D.C. He had gotten another job in Minneapolis, but he had promised his previous employers to finish out one last academic year. And so I had been home alone when autumn became winter, and winter became what the local weather people insisted on calling "Snowmageddon."

I had thought we were prepared. We had bought that snowblower, after all. But even when I had failed to get it to start, it didn't seem like the end of the world. Three hundred feet was a lot of driveway, but three inches of snow wasn't so bad.

Then nine more fell the next week. And another foot the week after that.

It was a lot of shoveling. It became my all-consuming hobby.

When the foot of snow fell overnight, that was the first time Oskar had motored over in his Bobcat and cleared out the heavy stuff from the end of my driveway. I had watched him shove it all across the road to the open field, spreading it as wide and flat as he could.

Like, I had thought at the time, a kid with a toy truck in a sandbox. Vroom, vroom.

He hadn't parked his Bobcat that time, just waved to get my attention. I had jogged out to the road to see what he wanted. This had been before the ice had coated everything, and jogging down the driveway was still a thing I could safely do.

"Don't let the snowbanks get too high," he had said.

I had wanted to crack a joke, but not having much experience with snow, I hadn't known what would be funny. So I had just nodded. I think I even thanked him for his advice, I'm not sure.

Mike came home for Christmas, but after not seeing him for months, and him only being home for less than two full weeks, I had completely forgotten about the snowblower I couldn't start.

Until the first time it snowed in January. Another nine inches. Just me and my trusty shovel.

And my neighbor in the Bobcat. He had cleared away the boulders for me, but that time he did park the Bobcat, cutting off the engine and getting out before telling me again, "don't let the snowbanks get too high."

I felt like he was speaking in some kind of code I wasn't getting.

"I'm trying not to," I said. "I forgot how much it snows here."

He blinked in a rare show of an emotion, or at least as much emotion as a blink can convey. It was surprise, anyway.

"You and your husband are from Washington, D.C." Again, not a question.

"He's a born and bred Virginian, and we were living in D.C. together for about ten years before moving out here, but you know, I'm from here originally."

"You're from here." He blinked again. More like confusion this time.

"I moved to Arlington in the middle of kindergarten. Right after the Halloween Blizzard of 1991. I'm sure you remember that one. Seems like people around here still talk about it. It broke my mother. She was from Virginia originally and demanded we move closer to her family. But my father's people are from around here," I said.

"Your people are from here."

"My father's father's family are all very German, from the Hanover area, but my father's mother's people were Norwegian immigrants who settled in St. Michael."

I had biked to both towns from our house during the summer. Just like where we were now, they had been farm towns in my grandparents' day, but were fast becoming exurbs now.

"My people are from St. Michael," Oskar said. A rare personal statement. I was almost overwhelmed by the sudden openness.

Then I realized I had missed the hidden question again. I was pretty sure that Oskar was old enough to be my grandfather, but I didn't want to say so out loud. He spent a lot of time outdoors. A lot of time. That aged people.

"Maybe you knew some of my relatives, then?" I said at last. "My grandmother's maiden name was Skogen."

Another blink, but this one I couldn't quite read. I wasn't absolutely sure it was one of recognition.

Then he drew in another long sigh before pointing at my snowbanks. "They are too high. A Skogen should know this."

And then he had just left me standing there, puzzling over what that could possibly mean.

As I hung up my shovel then bent to pry the cleats off the bottoms of my boots, I tried again to work out what he might have meant.

I had decoded the statements that were really questions in disguise. And I was starting to read some of what his slow blinks meant. But the sighs, clearly fraught with meaning, were still eluding me.

And if my Skogen had some great family lore about the height of snowbanks, it had clearly died out a generation or two before.

I woke the next morning to a sunny, not a cloud in the sky day. But when I went outside at noon to make my way to the mailbox, the air was still cold enough to freeze the entire lining of my respiratory system in one only half-aborted breath.

I zipped the collar of my parka up over my nose, checked the cleats on my boots, and started down the driveway to the mailbox. The first part wasn't too bad, but then it rarely was.

But the bottom half, under the gray branches of the trees that crossed skeletally bare overhead, it was exactly like a hockey rink. It was thick, yes, and in its heart it was still stained yellowish-brown from the road runoff. But the top layer was smooth like glass, polished to a shine.

Like someone had taken a mini-Zamboni to it in the night.

Even with my cleats, it was slow going. I had to slam my feet down pretty hard to get a grip, and I absolutely couldn't hurry.

But I finally made it out to the mailbox to find a few local flyers, something that looked like a personal card but would likely turn out to be junk mail, and another missed delivery card.

Sorry we missed you!

I looked back at the ice on the driveway. I had stopped ordering from online stores about a month before, and I had never been one for subscription services that delivered boxes of things. I had no idea what this package was, any more than I did about the card from the day before. I supposed it was just possible they were for the same package.

But I also really needed groceries. I had been eating out of what was stored in the chest freezer for a month, but even that was starting to run low. And I was getting heartily sick of freezer-burned peas. The grocery delivery driver would stop at the end of the driveway and text me to come get the bags myself. I knew that from prior experience, that is to say, my last four orders.

But this ice on the driveway was becoming a problem too big to be solved only in my spare time.

For the first time in five years, I called in sick to work. Then I headed back outside.

After ten minutes, I had to admit that even with its steel edge, the shovel was doing absolutely nothing. That layer of ice might as well be steel itself.

I tried a different shovel, one meant for gardening. Then I tried the edging tool Mike used to put the landscaping borders around my flowerbeds the spring before. Even that, nothing more than a flat edge of metal, did nothing.

But, to my complete surprise, the desperation play of stabbing at it with a pitchfork proved surprisingly effective.

A lot of work, but effective. It was immensely satisfying, seeing the sheets of ice break up into chunks I could heft up then hurl over the snowbanks. I felt like an Olympic discus thrower, if the discus in question was more the size of a sewer hole cover.

I might have been having a little too much fun. It certainly took a long time to notice that Oskar, Bobcat-less, was standing at the end of my driveway, watching me.

"It's the trees, right?" I said with a nervous laugh. "Too much shade here. Well, that and the driveway uphill gets more sun, so it runs off down here. At least, that's what I think is going on."

"That's what you think," he said.

I brushed bits of ice off my thick gloves and tried to find the question in that statement, but came up empty. I did briefly remember my first thought on encountering the ice that morning: that it had been smoothed over by a mini-Zamboni in the night. Because that was completely ludicrous, and nothing in any of my conversations with Oskar had ever hinted at any love of whimsy in him.

But the image lingered in my mind, silly as it was. Mainly, it was the way my repeated stabs with the shovel at the bottoms of the snowbanks were creating a sort of overhanging bit of snow over that layer of ice. There was a gap of air there. It almost made it look like the ice was flowing out from under the snowbanks in the night.

Which made no sense. The yard sloped away from the driveway. The driveway was higher ground. Water should flow the other way.

Shouldn't it?

"It has to be spring soon, right?" I said. It didn't come out anywhere near as cheery as I had meant it to. In D.C., the cherry trees might just be on the brink of full glorious blooming, but everything here was under ice. Even the fluffy snow was under a razor-sharp layer of ice. A boot could punch through, but that ice could still cut an ankle if it found one.

"I understood your grandmother's people were the Skogen family," Oskar said.

"That was my grandmother's people," I said, not quite snapping at him, but I was so, so close. "I was born in Robbinsdale, which I'm sure to you is practically the heart of downtown Minneapolis. And yes, I've been living in D.C. for longer than I care to count up just now. I'm a city girl. I admit it. Whatever snow lore my exalted family was keepers of, none of it was passed down to me. So I'm sorry, I have no idea what I'm not doing correctly here. Aside from piling my snowbanks too high. Which, quite frankly, I have no idea what else I'm supposed to do. How far do you think I can throw it? Or am I meant to shovel the driveway, then shovel the yard, too?"

I knew I was talking faster and louder by the second and forced myself to stop, fisting my gloved hands and forcing myself to take a breath.

But Oskar just let it all wash over him without a word. He watched without expression as I got myself back under control. Only then did he look up the road, to the point where our dead-end dirt road met the larger county road. We couldn't see anything from where we were but trees and snow, but I knew what he was directing his gaze toward.

The development that was getting underway on both sides of that county road. The corn fields had been plowed under, the dirt moved around to make smoother surfaces, the routes of future roads carefully marked out. As soon as the snow melted and spring began, they'd start digging to put in the sewer and utility accesses. Then the houses would spring up.

Mike and I had known it was coming when we bought the house. It wasn't in sight from our yard, so we didn't mind it much. After years of having so many neighbors on all sides of us, it wasn't really that traumatic.

But for our neighbors, I supposed it was a different matter. Aside from Mike and me, the people who were newest on the block had moved in thirty years ago.

And I was pretty sure Oskar had been here since pioneer days, or nearly.

"Lots of disruption lately," he said. "Tearing up the fields, displacing so many things. They are still looking for places to settle again."

"The exterminator said all the field mice we had in the fall were because of mowing down the fields," I said, although I hadn't known at the time if that was really true. I had never lived in the woods before. I had no idea what was normal for animals. Now I saw deer almost daily, skunks and raccoons occasionally in the evenings, and red-tailed hawks circling the skies all day long. Sometimes at night I could hear coyotes baying over their victorious hunts. Maybe they were displaced too.

But Oskar was gazing at me with such a weary look I was sure I was misunderstanding him again.

"What do I need to know?" I asked. It was the most direct question I could think of. He seemed like he'd prefer a direction question.

But all he said was, "you can't let the snow banks get so tall."

And then he left. Which was just as well. The torrent of words building up inside of me had a lot of impolite ones mixed in, and it was probably better if I kept those to myself.

But I nursed my anger. It was such good fuel for the back-breaking work I was still doing on the ice.

What was his obsession with the heights of snowbanks, anyway? It wasn't like there was any kind of homeowners' association on our street. Given that I had yet to even meet most of my neighbors, they were the very opposite of those kinds of people.

I remembered as a kid being warned never to build snow forts in the snowbanks left by the street plows, because they might collapse when the plow came by again. My childhood imagination had gone to town with that image, being trapped in a tunnel of snow when it all piled down on top of you. Then some huge metal blade pushed in to get you...

But I doubted that was what Oskar meant, either.

The afternoon was all too short, even for being technically spring-time. I broke up all the ice I could and had nearly reached the road before it was too dark to carry on. I tossed the last few chunks of ice over the snowbank.

Or at least I tried to. I was so exhausted, one skimmed along the top before sliding back down the driveway side, smashing into even smaller bits of ice that I decided not to try to clean up.

Another tipped as it spun, more like a ninja star, embedding itself in the snowbank. And not even close to the top. It was so close to the bottom I expected it too to smash all over the driveway. But in the end it just stuck there, quivering.

I hoisted my pitchfork and started the long climb back up my driveway. I was almost too tired to make it back inside. My whole body hurt. It was like I hadn't really noticed it while I was channeling my anger into breaking up the ice, but I definitely was noticing it now. I needed a hot bath.

And maybe an early bedtime, I added to myself as I hung up the pitchfork. Because I was so tired, I was starting to hallucinate sounds.

There was no way that snowbank had screamed when I had ninja-starred it with the sheet of ice. Or giggled at me when I had walked away.

I ran the water as hot as I could stand it, then sat back with a cloth over my eyes with a very different sort of sigh than my neighbor was constantly deploying. I expected at first I would have to be careful not to drift off to sleep in the water.

But then my brain started whirring, and by the time I got out of the bath to get dressed, I was no longer tired at all. Sore, sure, but not remotely ready for bed.

I had been trying to remember everything I could about my grand-mother Skogen, but she had died when I was pretty young. I had only one solid memory of her, from my first Christmas after we had moved from Minnesota to Virginia. She had come to visit, and we had made lefse together. Or she had made it and I had watched; I'm sure at six I hadn't been any help at all.

I don't think I'd had lefse since, but now I had a sudden craving.

Even more surprisingly, a quick inventory of my kitchen showed I had enough of the ingredients on hand to follow the recipe I found on the internet. Sure, I'd have to use powdered milk, and even more shockingly powdered potatoes. I clearly remembered my grandmother ricing those boiled potatoes herself. But I could at least give it a whirl.

I mixed everything up and formed it into balls, then let it chill in the fridge for a few hours. Not as long as it was supposed to, but this weird sense of urgency kept driving me to work faster. It had the same voice as the one that said that powdered potatoes would work well enough. Maybe not to be trusted, then, but I couldn't tune it out.

But while the balls of dough were chilling, I went down to the base-ment, to where I kept all the boxes I had never unpacked from our move from Virginia. I wasn't quite sure what I was looking for until I found it.

An open but almost entirely undrunk bottle of Brennivín. Mike and I had bought it during our Icelandic anniversary trip, waiting a year until our next anniversary to sample it.

And knowing instantly that neither of us cared for Brennivín. It sounded like it would be lovely, just a hint of caraway and lots of Iceland's pure glacial water. But I decided I preferred caraway in bread, and Mike agreed. And we had put the bottle away and forgot about it so completely we had packed and moved with it. I mean, if we'd spared it any thought at all, we would've poured it out and recycled the bottle rather than let it take up precious space in our already over-packed truck.

Bottle in hand, I went back upstairs to the kitchen. I pulled out the big electric griddle I used for making tortillas on Taco Tuesday and plugged it in, then found my rolling pin. I didn't have the sort of cover that my grandmother had put on hers that gave the lefse a rougher texture than tortillas, but I decided one of my tea towels would probably work if I was generous enough with the flour.

An hour later, completely covered in too-generous amounts of that flour, I had a stack of really-not-too-bad lefse. And a bottle of not-for-me-but-maybe-for-someone Brennivín.

I also had that voice in my head telling me to bring it all outside and share it around. Which seemed perfectly reasonable. No human being should eat an entire stack of lefse, but they were definitely better when they were hot and fresh.

I went into my cupboard and pulled out my entire stack of miniature bowls. I used them to measure out spices when I was cooking, and they only held a tablespoon or so each, but I had a lot of them.

I also, for reasons I could no longer remember, had entirely too many little dishes meant for dipping sauces or soy sauce or whatever. I had never yet had twelve dinner guests at once, but if I did, they'd better like to dip things.

I carried all this outside, not bothering with my coat or hat or even my boots and cleats. Just me, in my loungewear and house shoes, shuffling down that treacherous driveway in the dark at what had to be three in the morning.

But I didn't slip. Not even once.

I walked along the snowbank, stopping every few steps to set either a dipping dish full of bits of lefse or a spice bowl full of Brennivín on the snow. I went down one side of the driveway, then back up the other before I ran out of bowls.

I had also run out of Brennivín, so I tossed the empty bottle into the recycle bin outside the garage. But I still had half a piece of lefse left. It was no longer even remotely warm, but I ate it anyway.

That was the last thing I remembered. Standing alone in my driveway, munching on cold lefse, looking at the way the moonlight sparkled off the stainless steel of all those spice bowls, and saying to myself it was a good thing the alcohol wouldn't freeze.

I didn't know why that was a good thing. Or why I said, "Skål!"

And I don't remember finally going to bed.

But it was nearly noon when a harsh ringing woke me from a deep sleep. What was that sound? That annoying, and yet somehow so very, very welcome sound? It was familiar. I could almost place it…

The doorbell.

Someone was ringing my doorbell.

Someone had come up my driveway?

I ran to the door, but got there too late. Whoever had been there was gone now.

But they had left a package.

I picked it up and saw it had been delivered by the post office. They had come up the driveway?

I set it down just inside the door, then went outside. I was once again not dressed for the weather. Even less so this time; at least my loungewear was basically fleece. My pajamas were thin cotton, and the wind cut right through them.

And I was barefoot.

But I had to see. I couldn't wait to get dressed first.

I scampered down the driveway, hopping around like I used to do as a kid when running barefoot on the grass had briefly turned to running barefoot on hot pavement.

What was under my feet now was not hot, but it was definitely not ice. I was touching the driveway. Even down at the bottom, between the culvert and the road, it was all clear, ice-free driveway.

And there, exactly where I had left them the night before, were all my spice bowls and dipping dishes.

But not exactly *as* I'd left them. They were all empty now. I gathered them up as quickly as I could, then ran back to my house. I saw a blur of motion out of the corner of my eye and paused on one of the sunnier patches of driveway to return Oskar's wave.

He was too far away for me to see his face, not that I would've been able to read his expression even if I had. But I was pretty sure he had seen that my driveway was now clear. That had definitely been a "good job" sort of wave.

I went back into my house and immediately ran for my warmest pair of slippers and my fluffy bathrobe. Even cold as I was, I wasn't going to wait to get dressed before seeing what was in that box.

It had been Mike's handwriting on the address label. I had to know what he'd sent me. I had just seen him a few weeks before, and would see him again soon enough. What couldn't wait for him to give to me then?

I opened the box and the smell of cherries immediately filled my kitchen, mixing nicely with the lingering scent of lefse from the night before. I inhaled deeply, held it in my lungs like I could somehow hug the smell, then finally let my breath out again before looking inside the box.

It was filled with origami flowers. Some red, some white, but mostly pink.

No, not flowers. Cherry blossoms. Hundreds of them.

How long had Mike spent folding these?

It was a very non-Mike thing to do. I saw the card tucked down the side of the box and reached for it, sure it would be some explanation of how he had set his whole class to folding paper cherry blossoms for extra credit. Or just brownie points. He was a university professor, after all, not a schoolteacher.

Or maybe it was actual brownies. After the night I had just had, I wasn't taking anything off the table.

As I took a butter knife out of the drawer to cut open the card envelope, I heard another welcome and yet hard to recall sound. But this one was coming from outside.

I don't know one birdcall from another, but in my heart I decided what I heard outside my window was a robin. Because robins mean springtime. And that just had to be what I was hearing.

I set aside the card unread and headed to my desk to pull out my planner. I turned through the pages of the calendar until I reached the upcoming December. Then, after careful thought, I turned back two pages, just in case.

Sometimes it snows like crazy in October, after all.

I dug around for a working pen, then at the top of the month of October, I wrote "Buy Brennivín!!!" and underlined it five times. Then I circled it with a red felt-tip marker, just to be sure.

Next winter would not be like this one. Not if the Skogen in me had anything to say about it.

HEAT DEATH

met my old friend Chloe Summers at the trailhead, just by the heavy chain that blocked off the trail with its rusted and bullet-riddled sign clearly stating TRAIL CLOSED and KEEP OUT.

Humans lived in colonies on the moon as well as Mars, had two thriving space stations at Lagrange points with four more under construction, and routinely sent shuttles back and forth between all those locations. The technological leaps we'd made just in my lifetime were staggering, and many great minds assured us that the best was still yet to come.

But in my hometown in western Texas on the fringes of the Chihuahuan Desert, shooting rifles at signs was still a favorite pastime. And I wish I could say it was just the kids.

It was almost as if all the locals assumed the point of a sign was to be a target, not to convey information. I mean, if that sign had done its job, neither Chloe nor I would be there, about to hike out in the worst heat wave in meteorological history.

I turned off the engine, then took a second to soak in one last breath of air-conditioned air. Then I opened the door of my cruiser and stepped out into the late afternoon Texas heat. It hit me like a physical blow, like my whole body had just been punched by the super-heated air. My lungs protested the dryness as much as the heat, and the first few breaths were borderline painful.

But I adjusted. I may have spent the last decade working in other more urban police departments in cities much further north, but I had been born here. This place was still in my blood.

Although I would argue that the summers had gotten a lot more brutal while I'd been away.

Chloe wasn't a park ranger, but she worked in the visitor's center part-time, and was a regular on all the hiking trails. She was a petite woman, maybe a hundred and ten pounds sopping wet, but didn't look like a child. She was hard to miss, even from a distance, and all the locals knew her well.

She was already decked out in hiking gear, complete with a coating of reddish-gold desert dust. Some of that dirt was new, a light coating on her otherwise white shirt, but the dirt on her hiking boots had built up over years. She had her head down as she walked up to me, hands in her pockets, and I couldn't see her face past the wide brim of her hat. But I could hear the tense anxiety in her voice as she said, "Hey, Lidia. I hoped it would be you that came when I called it in."

"It's my day with the cruiser. But Foley and McCormick are waiting for permission from the park board to come in with a wagon," I said.

"Why wait? You know they'll say yes," Chloe said.

"You know why. The wheels of bureaucracy may turn slowly, but they have to turn first," I said.

"Hey, remember when our town had *three* cruisers?" she said as she followed me to the back of the sheriff's office's only car.

"It's funny the things you can't afford anymore when all your tax-paying citizens move up into space," I said drily.

"Or just go north," she said.

I let that comment pass. "How far in did you say you found him?" I asked her as I opened the cruiser's trunk and pulled my cooling vest out of its cooler.

"For the two of us in current conditions, it's going to be about an hour's walk," she said. She examined my clothing choices without saying a word, lingering the longest on my still new-looking boots. But she nodded to herself, and I guessed she'd given me a pass. "I have enough water for both of us if you didn't bring enough."

"This holds about two liters," I said. I was putting my lightweight shirt over the bright blue vest, so I pointed at the bottle-carrying back-pack with my elbow.

Chloe frowned at it, then frowned even more fiercely up at the sky. The sun was working its way towards setting, although that would take it another four hours or so to achieve. The sky around it was cloudless, but had a smeary grayish blue hazy color that no one would ever photograph for a tourism brochure. It just made everything feel that much hotter.

"I'll bring three, just in case," she said, and headed back to her own truck to adjust the contents of the backpack waiting for her on the open tailgate.

"I can handle this, Chloe," I said. "You don't need to nanny me."

"It never hurts to be over-prepared," she said as she shouldered her pack. She looked like a scrawny thing, and that pack was easily half her weight. But I had known her since grade school, and I had no doubts about what those thin little muscles could do. Plus, Chloe had no quit in her.

"I don't see anyone parked here but the two of us," I pointed out as we passed the sign and chain and started up the first gentle slope of the desert trail. Chloe set the pace, but I could see her watching me closely to be sure I could keep up.

I tightened the straps on my backpack so that it rode a little higher and matched her pace. Chloe wasn't the only one who didn't have any quit.

"It's possible he came in from one of the other trailheads, but this one is the closest. And I really don't think he made it any farther," Chloe said. "Well, you'll see when we get to him." Then she punched me hard in the arm and said, "Shuttle!"

I rubbed at my biceps and looked up into the hazy blue sky. I could just make out the contrail of a shuttle as it passed overhead. It was too high up to be landing in Houston or taking off from New Mexico. I guessed it was a European shuttle just starting to enter the atmosphere.

"Do kids here still do that?" I asked her. She shrugged and grinned sheepishly at me.

After barely a quarter of an hour, Chloe made us both stop walking to drink water. There was no shade to be had anywhere, but we both had wide-brimmed hats.

"How are you feeling?" Chloe asked between sips from her bottle. "Headache? Dizziness? Anything?"

"I'm fine, Chloe," I said. "You don't have to coddle me. I spent two decades here before I went up north, you know."

"I'm not coddling you. This is just protocol," she said. "And for the record, I'm not feeling any symptoms of heat exhaustion or heat stroke either. But don't get cute and try powering through instead of telling me something's up."

"No, I won't," I said.

Chloe narrowed her eyes at me, but she knew me better than anyone. She knew when my voice dropped down to that register I was being completely sincere. She accepted my answer with a nod. Then we stowed our bottles and carried on with the hike.

I had forgotten how beautiful the desert could be, even when it was so stinking hot that the animals were all tucked away out of sight. I could almost imagine we were on Mars, save for the sparse if sun-baked vegetation.

But something else had caught my eye, a flash of reflected light just off the trail. "What's that?" I asked.

Chloe spared it barely a glance. "Beer can. That's new. I'll pick it up on our way back out."

"What do you mean, it's new?" I asked.

"Lidia, come on. You know this trail is my special place. That beer can, like this man's body, wasn't here yesterday."

"But the trail is closed," I said.

"It's funny how a chain and a sign don't really keep people off the trail," Chloe said. "The park service does their best, but people take their own chances. If it makes you feel better, the beer drinkers usually come out after dark to look at the stars. That's a safer time for rule breaking. And you have to admit, the view out here at night is phenomenal."

She didn't have to rub it in. I remembered as well as she did the many nights we came out here after dark in high school. But it had only been Chloe who looked up at the sky, and it hadn't been the stars that captivated her. It had been the moon, the place she had been meant to be born and raised on, before her mother's accident had sent her back to Earth, both pregnant and in a coma. Chloe had a lot of disappointments in her life, and a lot of what-ifs she spent a little too much time speculating about.

But, as usual, I didn't say anything about that. I knew she never wanted advice from her friend with two living parents.

The beer can wasn't the only sign of people still using the closed trail, although when I started spotting the others after our second water break, I wished for more beer cans. Or better yet, traffic signs. Because without those, the things we started seeing riddled with bullets were small animals. Mostly lizards, but the occasional rock squirrels and desert cottontails.

"All this blood looks pretty fresh, doesn't it?" I said as we passed another rock sprinkled in reddish-brown spots. I could follow the trail to the body of the rabbit only a couple of meters away. "And this looks like more than a twenty-two."

"It's messed up," Chloe said, but didn't really look at what I was pointing to. I decided not to press her. I was used to dealing with dead bodies in my line of work, and while I was sure Chloe had seen more than her share of dead rabbits, I was also sure that finding a dead man had probably bothered her more than she was willing to show.

Still, the animal carnage was upsetting. What was wrong with people? Was it really just extreme heat and boredom?

"He's just past this hill," Chloe said as we stopped a third time for water. "I hope you're ready for this, because he's a mess."

"I've seen dead bodies before, Chloe," I told her. Not that I'd tell her any more about what I'd seen than that. It was enough that I had to live with some of it.

"I guess. But his smell has to be unique," she said. She put her bottle away, but the look on her face was still pensive. Then she said, "Do you remember in grade school when we made mummies out of chickens from the grocery store?"

"Yeah," I said. Chloe and I had been science partners, but Chloe had been so grossed out by all of it that I had done all the work. I well remembered the feel of that muscle tissue as it got more and more tough and leathery each time I had wiped away the old salt and packed the body again in the new.

But I remembered the smell too. It hadn't been anything like the smell of fried chicken. It had just smelled like a dry, dead thing.

Five minutes later, when I was finally standing over the body, I had to agree. He smelled just like that chicken. If you had enough heat, you didn't need salt to make a mummy, apparently.

"Lidia, I think I've seen him enough. Do you mind if I just go up to that rock outcropping and keep an eye out for your boys?"

"Don't let Foley and McCormick hear you call them boys," I said as I gave her a wave of permission. I heard her footsteps over the rougher off-path terrain, but I was already in investigation mode, examining and photographing the ground all around the body for possible clues before I approached it any closer.

Like the heat, I needed a minute to adjust to that smell.

The man had fallen face-down right in the middle of the path, like he'd tripped over an exposed bit of rock and then never gotten up again. I found the rock that was likely to blame, but the erosion of the soil around it had happened over years of time, not suddenly and recently.

Well, when Chloe had called me, she had been sure this was just an accident. It was just my training to treat every death as a homicide. It might not have been the way my predecessor had run things, but it was my way.

"He's not local?" I called up to Chloe.

"Never seen him before in my life," Chloe shouted back.

And yet there'd been no car parked at the trailhead.

But as I got closer to the body, I realized that wasn't even the start of the strange things.

Every stitch of clothes on the man's body was brand new. The treads on the bottoms of his top-of-the-line hiking shoes were almost completely unworn. There was a quality control sticker still attached to the back bottom hem of his sun protective shirt. His wide-brimmed hat was uncreased save for the hefty fold he was putting into it now, half-crushed under his head.

He looked for all the world like he had gone into a sporting goods store and asked them to outfit him for a hike. And then he'd come straight out here in all his spanking new gear.

This wasn't a trail for beginners in *good* weather.

So why had he come out here during a heat wave when the trail was closed to even experienced and prepared hikers?

I took pictures of everything, then flipped back the loose folds of the sun protective shirt. Underneath it he was wearing a cooling vest just like the one I was, although it had the flat, squishy look of a vest full of melted cooling packs. But there was no sign of moisture or even dirt that had been muddied then dried again under him. None of those packs had burst.

So he hadn't been shot or stabbed, so far as I could see.

I heard footsteps running up to me just before Chloe said, "Your boys are nearly here."

I was about to correct her word choice again, but just as I was about to abandon my examination of the ground under the body, I saw something odd.

"What's that?" I asked. It was meant to be rhetorical, but Chloe leaned in behind me, blocking out the sun.

It was the corner of some sort of plastic pouch, but I had no idea what it was the corner of. It didn't look like modern plastics at all. More like something from the 60s or 70s. Way before my time, but I've been to a museum or two in my day.

"I'll tell you what I don't see," Chloe said from behind me. "I don't see any water. Like, not even an empty bottle."

"What time did you find him?" I asked as I used the end of a stylus to poke at the plastic pouch thing.

"It was an hour and a half before I found you," she said. I wasn't looking at her, but I knew from the tone of her voice that if I glanced up at her, I'd see her squinching her whole face up tight. It was what she always did as a kid when she knew she was about to get into trouble.

"You were out here in the middle of the day?" I asked. Then I stepped back from the body to stand up, turn, and look at her. Yep. It was a milder squinch than she'd had in grade school, but it was definitely still there. And a little off-putting in a thirtysomething woman. But that was Chloe.

"I know this place better than anyone," she said.

"I can think of a park ranger or two who might argue with you on that one," I said.

"I know my limits better than anyone," she said, straightening her spine to bring her to her full, not terribly impressive height.

But I had to admit, she was right. Chloe didn't overestimate herself, ever. She might underestimate herself on occasion, but never the other way around.

Still. "You were out here without a buddy," I said.

"Sat phone," she said, slapping the thigh pocket on her cargo shorts. "If something happens that is so terrible I can't make a call, a buddy is only there to lead everyone to my corpse."

Then she flinched a little, not quite looking at the corpse right beside the two of us.

"Fine," I said, letting that go. "And you said you were out here yesterday. What time?"

"This point of the trail? Sunset. Ish," she said with a vague waggle of her hand.

I clicked my tongue as I thought it through. "If he started hiking this morning before ten or so, it was only in the low eighties. He might've thought he could handle it."

I looked down at the corpse again, but past the clothes to the body itself. He actually looked like he had been in pretty good shape. Solidly middle age, but nice muscle tone. Although I got the sense that under the sunburn he might've been really quite pale. There were a few spots under his hat or under his chin that looked pasty, but it was hard to get a good look without moving the body.

"The trail was closed for a reason," Chloe said with a sigh. "We don't have the staffing to post guards."

I heard the sound of an electric motor approaching and knew Foley and McCormick were close.

"It's going to be a wait for the medical examiner to get here," I said with a frustrated sigh of my own. "He covers twelve counties, and eleven of them are more populous than ours."

"Does it matter? I mean, this was pretty clearly an accident," Chloe said.

"Maybe," I said.

But I really wanted to know who this man was.

———

It sucked sharing one medical examiner with eleven other counties, but on the upside, our ME was legitimately good at his job. Like me, Marco Villalobos was from the area but had gone north to first get his doctorate and then stayed there because that's where the decent-paying jobs were. Unlike me, he hadn't come back home until he retired.

But retirement didn't suit him. After less than a month, he started volunteering to help our previous ME. But that woman had *not* been good at her job. The local police departments had been complaining about her for years, but it only took Marco three months to put together enough evidence to have her convicted of an impressive array of crimes, from fraud to abuse of a corpse. Since then, he'd been working alone, for far less than he'd been getting paid back in Chicago.

It took a long time to get reports back from him. Sometimes it took months. But we could rely on his findings, and they held up in court. In a cash-strapped county, that was the best we could hope for.

This time, it did indeed take three weeks before Marco could get around to autopsying our victim. And I had to drive four counties over to his lab to talk to him about it.

But in my mind, it was worth it. Especially when the first thing he told me was the answer to my most puzzling question.

"The polyurethane is in pretty good shape, especially given what it's been through recently. But it's not an antique, just a very good replica," he said, showing me the evidence bag that contained the strange plastic pouch. I had gotten a full view of it three weeks before, after Foley and McCormick had loaded the body onto the wagon, but that had only raised more questions in my mind.

It was shaped like a chunky L, rather like a map of the state of Louisiana. And it had a PVC tube running down the inner curve to the bottom. There were patches of Velcro on the top and down one side.

"A replica what?" I asked. There was a betting pool back at the sheriff's office. The most votes were for colostomy bag, but, like, a really old colostomy bag.

"You've never been to Space Center Houston?" he asked me, but didn't wait for a response. "This is called an IDB. In-suit drinkbag. It would attach to the HUT with those Velcro patches. HUT means hard upper torso assembly."

"Why did this man have this bag?" I asked.

"I agree it's not the usual choice of water conveyance in the desert," he said. "You already ID'd the victim."

That wasn't a question; he knew I had. But it hadn't told me much. "His name was Brant Taylor, fifty-five years old, born and raised on the moon. And that's about as far as I've gotten. Have you dealt with lunar bureaucracy before?"

"Yes, I have," he said with sympathy. "If it helps, I didn't get much more than that with my own records requests. Date of birth, but no place of birth more specific than 'moon'."

"No employment history or anything," I said.

"Oh, he was a recluse," Marco said airily.

"How do you know that?" I asked.

"I have a friend who retired to a dome on the edge of the Sea of Tranquility," he said. "Unlike me, he didn't want anything to do with the medical field anymore. He runs a bar that caters to… well, we jokingly call them moon truckers. You know, the drivers who haul cargo between the domes."

"Brant Taylor was a moon trucker?" I asked. But that didn't track with the clothes he had been wearing. Even the hiking pants that Marco must have cut off of his body had cost more than I made in a week.

That was setting aside the cost of the shuttle from the moon to Houston. People who went into space saved up for decades to make the trip. And few ever came back.

"No, no," Marco said. He took the evidence bag from me, as if he still found the IDB fascinating. But at nearly eighty, he could actually remember a time when only a select few ever went up into space. And those few were idolized as heroes.

"He must have had access to quite a bit of money," I said. Marco set the evidence bag aside and reached for the tablet with his notes on it.

"He was a financial speculator. Which would mean he had connections to Earth banks and stock markets, if you really need to dig into him outside of the world of lunar bureaucracy," Marco said. "No, he wasn't a moon trucker. But the truckers all knew him because he would hire them to bring things out to his own private dome. He paid very, very well. But even so, no one wanted those jobs."

"Really," I said.

"He could afford to be an eccentric, and he went all in," Marco said. "He paid well, but he made you earn it. And few thought it was a fair exchange in the end. I suppose the only real mystery is how he ended up dead here and not killed in his own dome by someone in his employ."

"No family, then?" I asked.

"No, lunar records would've passed on marriage records and any birth certificates where his name was on file as the father," Marco said.

"They didn't mention they even looked," I grumbled.

"No, they don't like to be forthcoming with information. If you deal with them enough, you get a sense for what's being said by what they *aren't* telling you."

"Thanks for the tip, but I really hope to never deal with them again," I said.

Given that the population of my county was dwindling year after year, that felt like a pretty safe bet.

"I'm guessing we found the same travel info on him?" Marco said as he scanned his notes.

"He took a shuttle down to Houston, but had an open return ticket. So he planned to return, but didn't know how long he'd be stateside," I said.

"That's not unusual," Marco said. "Usually it's for medical reasons. Someone who's been living off Earth for more than a year can have a variety of adverse events that can't always be predicted. An open ticket is more about wanting the option to get home in a hurry because of medical reasons than it is about delaying the return for other reasons."

"I'm guessing the moon is the worst, because of the gravity difference," I said.

"And you would be right," Marco said. "But this Brant Taylor was exceptionally prepared to come to Earth. He had maintained muscle tone and bone density through exercise, diet, and I'm guessing various medications that likely weren't cheap. He was in tiptop shape."

Which wasn't surprising. I had thought as much when I'd looked at him before. But also, I had gotten the strong impression he had thought he could handle that hike.

But hiking in general and hiking in the middle of a record-setting heat wave were two very different propositions.

"Why was he here?" I pondered out loud.

"Here on Earth or here in our little corner of it?" Marco asked. "Either is a puzzler, really. As good of shape as he was in, and all the effort he must've made to stay in that shape, fifty-five is a really late age to decide to come back to see the homeland. I can tell by the patterns of his bone growth that he's been in top shape his whole life. He didn't get a sudden drive to see Earth and then start the appropriate regimen."

"But he did come here. And he bought a new outfit, walked out into the desert, and died in it," I said. "We never found any other luggage, or a vehicle, or anything. But we do know he wasn't dressed like that when he got off the shuttle in Houston."

We could hear voices outside the office door, two people coming up a hall that only led to the room we were in.

"Right," Marco said, turning back to his tablet one last time. "Cause of death is heat stroke and dehydration. There's no question about that. And he wasn't cuffed or tied up or anything. I know you'll need evidence of something to keep investigating this as a homicide, but I don't have it to give you. Sorry."

"I know," I said. But I hated it. From a budgetary standpoint, I really did have to set this case aside. It looked like accidental death, or death by misadventure, or whatever.

But I still had so many questions.

"If your friend learns any more, will you have him pass it on to me?" I asked.

"I'll let him know, but I wouldn't get your hopes up," he said. "Recluse, remember?"

"Right. Recluse."

But I couldn't let it go at that.

———

I had a lot of time to think on the drive back home. But those thoughts weren't great. I came to a conclusion before I'd even gotten out of the ME's parking lot, but that just left too much time to agonize over the ramifications.

Because there was only one thing that connected my hometown with the moon. And the minute I remembered that little fact, everything else started lining up so neatly.

When I got back to town, I didn't turn in to the sheriff's office or even head home.

I went first to the home of Hector and Bonnie Summers. They were technically Chloe's grandparents, but given the fact that spot for "father" on Chloe's birth certificate had been left blank, and her mother had never recovered from the coma that had gotten her removed from the moon, it would be more appropriate to just call them her parents.

I had spent roughly half my childhood in this little suburban home with its ring of junipers all around it, not quite protecting the always peeling paint from the rays of the sun. They were the variety called drooping junipers because they always looked like they were half-dead from lack of water, all wilted and shriveled. But they looked particularly bad this year.

I knocked on the door, trying not to notice how badly the boards of the deck under me were sagging under my weight. The whole place was in need of repairs that I knew the Summers couldn't afford.

When no one answered my first knock, I knocked again. Then I took a few steps back, off the porch and onto the scrabby, parched lawn. I was trying to see if there was any movement behind the upstairs windows, but was momentarily distracted by the sight of another shuttle contrail arcing across the sky. It was a cleaner blue today, not so hazy.

"Shuttle," I said to myself. But there was nobody close enough to punch.

I guess it was a little weird to be homesick now that I was home again. But you couldn't see shuttles in the skies over Chicago or Milwaukee.

Nostalgia. That's what I was feeling. I had come back to the place I knew, but I hadn't come back to the same time.

"Lidia? Lidia Alvarez?"

It was Hector, standing in the doorway in the shadows of the porch.

"Yes, it's me, Grandpa Hector," I said, and came up the steps to plant a kiss on his badly shaven cheek. He was shorter than I remembered, and grayer, but the bright blue eyes that were sparkling at me were as sharp as ever.

"Bonnie is going to be sorry she missed you, but she had the car drive her to the Wal-Mart. You know they closed the one in town, so it's a thirty-minute drive now," he said chidingly. Like it was my fault the local economy was dying.

Well, maybe he meant to make me feel guilty for not stopping by sooner. But my first three months on the job had been more hectic than I had expected. And that had been even before the dead body.

"I'm sorry I haven't been by," I said. "And I'm even more sorry that I'm not here now just to pay you a visit. You're both like family to me, and you deserve better from me."

Hector made a sort of sound of protest at my words, but motioned for me to follow him into Bonnie's sitting room. He shuffled slowly but steadily, his hand resting on the back of the sofa as he skirted it towards his old, familiar chair. He wasn't leaning on it, but he clearly wanted to know the support was there if he should need it. The fabric across the top of the sofa was worn smooth and shiny from all the times his hand had passed over it before.

As badly maintained as the outside of the house looked, everything in the sitting room was immaculate. The plethora of porcelain figures gleamed dust-free on shelves of brightly polished wood, and every-thing was decked in snowy white squares of lace that I knew Bonnie crocheted herself.

I hovered near Hector in case he needed a hand getting into his chair, but not so close that he could see me doing it. Once he was safely settled—without my help—I sank into the chair next to him.

"Not a visit, you say?" Hector said, digging around the items stacked on the end table beside his chair until he found a pair of glasses. They magnified his eyes to twice their normal size, but from the way his face suddenly relaxed, I realized he had been squinting at me without them.

"I had a few questions to ask you about a case," I said.

"The man in the park," Hector said with a sad nod.

"You know why I'm asking you about it?"

"I suppose if it was just because Chloe found him, you'd be talking to Chloe," he said. "Which means he is who I was afraid he was. The man from the moon."

"Do you know his name?" I asked, still hoping against hope that my hunch was wrong.

But Hector just shook his head. "No, we were never allowed to know his name. His lawyers made sure of that. We never got a penny towards Maria's medical care, or for Chloe, who was deprived of her mother in every way that matters. We never got anything at all."

I braced myself for tears or maybe anger, but Hector just bowed his head as if all he felt were crushing exhaustion.

"You know, Bonnie and I had reconciled ourselves to not having children. We were both past forty before Maria came along. Did you know that?"

"No, I didn't," I said. Although I probably could've guessed it. They were closer to seventy than sixty when I'd first met them. On Chloe's and my first day of kindergarten.

"As tragic as it was, what happened on the moon, Bonnie and I always saw the blessing in it. We thought we'd never have a single child. But in the end, we got to raise two."

I let that statement sit for a moment. The central air kicked on, and a vent I hadn't noticed that was right by my foot blasted my ankle with icy air.

I crossed my legs away from the vent, then leaned in towards Hector. "I remember when we were kids, you collected astronaut memorabilia."

"I did," he said, but the look on his face was bemused. He had no clue why I was bringing it up now. "I had to sell most of it. Well, all of it that was worth anything."

"That's a shame. I remember all the models you had of the rockets. They were to scale with each other. The Saturn V was huge!"

"Yes, yes," Hector said with a chuckle. But his eyes were worried about where this was going.

"Did you keep everything you couldn't sell?" I asked.

"Most of it," he said. But he was starting to sound like he was hedging now.

"What about authentic historical artifacts? Didn't you have a few of those? I remember mission patches and things like that."

Hector looked down at the hands folded on his lap. Then he looked up at me. "I think, Lidia, it would be best if you just asked me what you want to know. Stop dancing around it."

"You had a replica of a water pouch from an Apollo-era space suit," I said. "They called it an IDB. But it wasn't real. It was a very convincing fake."

"It was one of the things I couldn't sell," he said.

"So you still have it?" I asked.

He licked at his lips as if he suddenly found them dry. Then he said, "If you like, we can go out to the garage and have a look. But it's over a hundred and ten degrees in there, and there are a lot of boxes up in those rafters."

"All right," I said. He had a point; I didn't want to go digging through boxes in his furnace of a garage.

But I didn't really need to. "Did Chloe know it was there?"

"She helped me put it there. So, yes," Hector said. Then he put a hand to his forehead and leaned against the arm of his chair. But after a moment he shifted that hand to covering his eyes.

"I guess you know what I suspect," I said.

"I guess I do," he said.

"I have to go find Chloe now. I truly am sorry."

He didn't speak at first, and I suspected behind the cover of that hand he was weeping.

But his voice was as steady as ever as he said, "She has a shift at the visitor center today. She'll be there until six."

"Thank you," I said. But I had to add, "I trust you won't call her to tell her I'm coming?"

"No, no," he said, shaking his head but still not dropping the hand from over his eyes. "No, if you think she did this, then you have proof. And if she did it, then she has to take the consequences."

"I'm sorry you never found any justice the first time around," I said. "That wasn't right."

"No, and this doesn't make it better," he said.

I had to leave him there alone with his grief, unsure of how long it would take before Bonnie would be home. But then they'd just be grieving together.

They were about to lose another daughter. But while the first one had died without ever coming out of the coma, at least this one might someday make it out of prison again.

Not in their lifetimes, though.

I sucked in a deep breath to fight down the threat of tears, then started my car and drove out to the visitor's center.

I arrived just as Chloe was locking the doors. She had her backpack on, water bottles full and sat phone in her pocket, I was sure. Her wide-brimmed hat was blocking me from her view at first, and I had to step into her path before she saw me.

She smiled at first, her usual toothy greeting. But something in my own face gave me away. And I watched as she just wilted. Her hands slipped from their grip on her backpack straps and dangled uselessly at her sides, her shoulders slumped, and her head dipped forward until all I could see was the top of her hat.

"Can I at least tell you why?" she asked. She was sniffling back tears, but she wasn't ginning up fake sobs in a bid for sympathy.

"He killed your mother," I said. "Effectively." It had taken her fifteen years to die, after all.

"Well, obviously," Chloe said, looking up at me with a little of her old fire back in her eyes. "I meant, why I lured him here."

"Because you couldn't afford to go to him on the moon," I said. As she would say, *obviously*, because even her mother had only made it to the lunar colony by winning a lottery on top of having an in-demand skill set as an electrician.

"Jesus, Lidia," Chloe said with that frustration only an old friend can have with another. "You are the master of the obvious."

"You'd be surprised how often that's all you need when it comes to the reasons why people kill," I shot back at her with a little irritation of my own.

"He claimed it was an accident, that it could've happened to anyone, but there was a reason he had his lawyers remove his name from everything. Because he knew it wasn't true!"

"I understand that he was a problematic employer," I said.

"More than that! Do you know he lured her out there with the promise of twice her usual weekly rate for a single day of work?" Chloe asked.

"That's not against the law," I said.

"He insisted that her wiring was to blame for a buzz in his dome-wide comms. Even though there was no way it could've been," Chloe went on.

"Again, not against the law."

"He refused to pay her if she didn't stay and fix the problem. Which she did. It took her hours, but she did it."

I didn't speak. I just waited for Chloe to go on.

She took a few deep breaths to get her growing anger back under her control. Then she said, "He put her on a two-person transport he had in his dome airlock, but he refused to drive her. She was supposed to ride in it while it was on autopilot mode to drop her off at the main dome, then go back to his dome on its own."

"Then what happened?" I had never gotten these details before. It had just been described as an accident, and nothing more was ever said.

And I had never asked. She had called herself a miracle baby, but always said it with such bitterness. I could see that the pain it caused

Chloe never diminished with time, so I was always careful to skirt conversations away from it.

But I was regretting that now. As painful as it would've been, I really wished I had pressed her more when I had the chance.

Before Chloe's anger had gotten the better of her. Before she had done things that couldn't be undone.

"The transport broke down. Obviously." That time, she really did roll her eyes at me. "And he refused to answer her calls for aid. And the main dome said it was out of their jurisdiction. So she had to get into the emergency suit on her own and walk it."

"She must've had the training," I said.

"Yes, yes. It's required to emigrate up there. But she'd only been there a week. She'd never actually operated a suit in a real vacuum. And now she had to do it with no backup."

"No buddy," I said, mostly to myself. Then I asked her, "Was it a faulty suit?"

"No, of course not," she said, throwing up her hands as if disgusted with how I kept missing her point. "He was found not to be at fault. Because as much as his transport had broken down, he had had all the correct emergency gear in place and fully operational."

"It was her error," I guessed.

"She shouldn't have been out there alone!" Chloe said. "That's on him. She bumped something and screwed up her air mix and was too hypoxic to fix it, but that's on him. It took too long for the dome to send out emergency workers to retrieve her after she triggered her distress button, but that's still. On. Him."

"So you sent him out into the desert alone," I said.

"I couldn't duplicate the experience exactly, of course," she said, and she was back to slumped defeat again. "I brought him to the sporting goods store after I picked him up from the spaceport in Houston. I showed him just what to buy. The best of the best."

"But you didn't buy him any water bottles," I said.

"If he would've asked, I would've told him what to get," Chloe said. "I told myself before he got here that I was going to play fair."

"Giving him that replica of an antique was playing fair?"

"I gave it to him when we got to the trailhead. I filled it with water and handed it to him, and asked him if he felt like he needed anything else. And he said no."

"It was still in the seventies," I guessed.

"It was 78 when we started," she said. But she had gone all tone-less, like she was already dead inside. "It was 112 when he finally collapsed."

"Why did he do it?" I asked.

"He came here because I said I had proof of his crimes," Chloe said. "Not his chief crime, ironically. But he had done some illegal things with his investment funds. And I had the receipts. All he had to do to buy my silence was come down to Earth and meet with me."

"How did you--?" I started to ask.

"It's actually about the fourth thing I've tried," Chloe said with the saddest laugh I've ever heard. "I tried romancing him, pretending to be a long-lost relative, offering him lush job opportunities. This was the first time he took the bait."

"Did you have--?"

"Of course not. But he must've done something illegal, since he came all the way down here to buy my silence," Chloe said.

I couldn't argue with that logic.

Which left me with just two more questions.

"Did he know who you were?"

"Not until I told him. Which wasn't until we were at the trailhead."

There was something ominous in her tone, and I knew the answer to my last question was going to break my heart.

But I had to get the words out.

"Chloe, how did you get him to walk, and to keep walking?"

"A gun. I don't have a gun on me now," she rushed to add, hands held high to show me they were empty. "I took Hector's hunting rifle out of his gun cabinet. I doubt he's even noticed it's missing. It's at my house. I wasn't going to put a murder weapon back in his house."

"He didn't miss it before," I said. "But I have a feeling he's noticed it now."

"You went to see him?"

"I did," I admitted. "How many of those dead animals along the trail were yours?"

"He didn't believe I could shoot him if he ran away," Chloe said. "He kept trying to test me. I could've shot him, but I didn't want him to die that way. But he wouldn't stop trying."

Then she finally broke down, hands over her face as she fell to her knees.

I had to pull her to her feet to walk her to the cruiser.

But her tears ended as quickly as they began, and she stood calmly beside me as I opened the back door and took her elbow to guide her inside.

"Lidia, shuttle," she said.

And I looked up. But she didn't punch my arm this time. Chloe was finally letting the past go.

I just wished she'd done it sooner.

SCI-FI SERIAL PODCAST!

Check out my new monthly podcast of serialized science fiction: THE TALES OF THE CHAI MAKHANI TRIO!

Elyot loathes the massive Commonwealth ships that hover menacingly over his home world of Adghal. He hates the Commonwealth enforcers who harass the populace even more. But with his mother missing and presumed dead, Elyot keeps his head down and strives to avoid notice. And he succeeds until the day two strangers enter his life...

New episodes of this sci-fi serial drop every 1st of the month.

Now streaming on Apple Podcasts, Google Podcasts, Spotify, Stitcher and more. Also available in eBook and print everywhere books or sold. For a complete episode listing, check out the page on my website.

COMPLETE SERIES: THE TRAVELS OF SCOUT SHANNON

The complete six-book series THE TRAVELS OF SCOUT SHANNON begin with book one, *Under Falling Skies*.

Scout Shannon's whole family died the day the Space Farers dropped an asteroid on their domed city. Now she lives alone, out in the wild with only her dogs for company. She prefers it that way.

But Scout finds herself at a crossroads. One road leads back to a quiet life snug under the protective dome of a city. The other road leads to a life in the rebellion, a life of adventure and excitement but also danger. Dare she try to find the rebels hiding in the hills?

Then a chance encounter with a stranger from the other side of the galaxy threatens to derail what remains of Scout's life. The entire galaxy awaits her, if she survives the next four days.

Under Falling Skies, a young adult science fiction novel, set on a remote planet with a distinctly Old West feel. For fans of gunslinging women and young girl assassins. And dogs.

Under Falling Skies, the first book in THE TRAVELS OF SCOUT SHANNON, available everywhere now.

COMPLETE SERIES: THE RITCHIE AND FITZ SCI-FI MURDER MYSTERIES

The complete six-book series THE RITCHIE AND FITZ SCI-FI MURDER MYSTERIES starts with *Murder on the Intergalactic Railway*.

For Murdina Ritchie, acceptance at the Oymyakon Foreign Service Academy means one last chance at her dream of becoming a diplomat for the Union of Free Worlds. For Shackleton Fitz IV, it represents his last chance not to fail out of military service entirely.

Strange that fate should throw them together now, among the last group of students admitted after the start of the semester. They had once shared the strongest of friendships. But that all ended a long time ago.

But when an insufferable but politically important woman turns up murdered, the two agree to put their differences aside and work together to solve the case.

Because the murderer might strike again. But more importantly, solving a murder would just have to impress the dour colonel who clearly thinks neither of them belong at his academy.

Murder on the Intergalactic Railway, the first book in THE RITCHIE AND FITZ SCI-FI MURDER MYSTERIES.

NEW SERIES: THE FORGOTTEN PLANET

THE FORGOTTEN PLANET, the new YA sci-fi adventure series fro
Kate MacLeod, starts with *Raiding the Forgotten Derelict.*

History sleeps beneath them all, but only she sees it.

Lafayette Eloi always knew her parents thought differently from
others. They kept their books buried beneath her mother's house. They
spoke an old language in the dead of night, whispering behind closed
doors and bolted shutters. She grew up in a village where no one was
related to her, and she never knew why.

Then, after her mother died, her father came to fetch her. Now she
and her mother's dog assist her father in his work. The work discussed
in whispers in the dark. The work that had cost Lafayette so much all
her young life.

But now she learns just how much her father's work means to their
entire world. Only no one knows anything about it. Only her father.
And only Lafayette.

Because the work that consumed her father's entire life and her
mother's too now nibbles at the fringes of Lafayette's own life. And
she cannot refuse its call.

Raiding the Forgotten Derelict, the first book in the new YA sci-fi
adventure series THE FORGOTTEN PLANET

ALSO FROM KATE MACLEOD

Love heists and capers? Then check out my new series, THE VIC HARPER CAPERS. The action starts with the novella *The Third Pole Job*.

Vic Harper and her gang retired wealthy from their life of thievery and heists. Whether in a luxury condo overlooking the river in Minneapolis or in a modernist mansion built into the side of a mountain in Colorado, life comes easy now.

Perhaps too easy.

When an old friend asks for a favor his niece, Vic and her mentor Chase Woodward leap at the chance to relieve a little of the boredom. But a quick bit of B&E in a wealthy suburb of Chicago leads to an even greater challenge.

The prize? Nothing much. Just the opportunity to level a playing field for their friend's niece.

But the heist? May prove to be their toughest ever. Because to get to the prize, they'll have to climb a mountain.

And not just any mountain. Their prize waits on the summit of Mount Everest.

The Third Pole Job, the first novella in THE VIC HARPER SERIES series. For those who love capers, heists and other impossible missions.

ALSO FROM RATATOSKR PRESS

Also from Ratatoskr Press, The Witches Three Cozy Mystery Series by Cate Martin, a mix of mystery and magic that begins with Book 1: Charm School.

Amanda Clarke thinks of herself as perfectly ordinary in every way. Just a small-town girl who serves breakfast all day in a little diner nestled next to the highway, nothing but dairy farms for miles around. She fits in there.

But then an old woman she never met dies, and Amanda was named in her will. Now Amanda packs a bag and heads to the big city, to Miss Zenobia Weekes' Charm School for Exceptional Young Ladies. And it's not in just any neighborhood. No, she finds herself on Summit Avenue in St. Paul, a street lined with gorgeous old houses, the former homes of lumber barons, railroad millionaires, even the writer F. Scott Fitzgerald. Why, Amanda can practically hear the jazz music still playing across the decades.

Scratch that. The music really, literally, still plays in the backyard of the charm school. Because the house stretches across time itself. Without a witch to protect this tear in the fabric of the world, anything can spill over. Like music.

Or like murder.

The complete series is out now, and it all starts with Charm School.

NEWSLETTER SIGNUP!

Like exclusive, free content?

To get two prequel short stories to THE RITCHIE AND FITZ SCI-FI MURDER MYSTERIES as well as a bonus prequel novelette to the completed six-book series THE TRAVELS OF SCOUT SHANNON, signup for my monthly newsletter at KateMacLeodWrites.com.

Thank you!

ABOUT THE AUTHOR

Photograph © 2016 Jonathan Conklin

Kate MacLeod has written stories which have appeared in *Analog*, *Strange Horizons* and *Mythic Delirium*, among other places. She is also the author of three young adult science fictions series: *The Travels of Scout Shannon*, *The Ritchie and Fitz Sci-Fi Murder Mysterie*s and *The Forgotten Planet*. She also contributes to a serialized science fiction podcast called *The Tales of the Chai Makhani Trio*. She currently lives in Minneapolis, Minnesota.

Find out more about the author and sign up for her newsletter at KateMacLeodWrites.com.

ALSO BY KATE MACLEOD

Novels

The Slums of the Solar System:

Mitwa

The Mars of Malcontents

The Whole World for Each

Books 1-3 Box Set

The Travels of Scout Shannon:

Under Falling Skies

In Quaking Hills

Among Treacherous Stars

Against Impassable Barriers

Over Freezing Altitudes

At Galactic Central

The Travels of Scout Shannon Books 1-3

The Travels of Scout Shannon Books 4-6

The Travels of Scout Shannon Books 1-6

The Ritchie and Fitz Sci-Fi Murder Mysteries:

Murder on the Intergalactic Railway

Murder in the Skies

Body in the Catacombs

Death on the Summit

An Undiplomatic Murder

A Lethal Betrayal

Sci-Fi Novellas

The Intergenerational Tree

I Rise into a Daybreak

Caper Novellas

The Third Pole Job

The Twelve Days of Christmas Job

10-Story Collections

Tales of Blood and Ink

Tales of Old Gods and New

5-Story Collections

Tales from Heian-Kyo and Others

Tales from the Edges and Ends

Tales from Forgotten Days

Tales from Ancient and Future Times

Tales From Across Space